Maxwell Gray

The Last Sentence

A Novel: Vol. I.

Maxwell Gray

The Last Sentence
A Novel: Vol. I.

ISBN/EAN: 9783337044169

Printed in Europe, USA, Canada, Australia, Japan

Cover: Foto ©Andreas Hilbeck / pixelio.de

More available books at **www.hansebooks.com**

THE LAST SENTENCE

A Novel

By
Maxwell Gray

Author of
'The Silence of Dean Maitland'

In Three Volumes
Vol.I.

London
William Heinemann
1893

THE LAST SENTENCE

PART I.

CHAPTER I.

BROCELIANDE.

THE bleak sandy waste was very still—so still that the dry bells of last year's heather kept their steady poise without the faintest quiver; the sunbeams were away; the vast gray canopy of clouded sky absorbed all lesser shades into its heavy darkness; only insects and creeping heath creatures stirred unseen; birds and rabbits were hidden in tufts of bramble and whin.

But overhead, brown against the slaty

gray, a hawk wheeled slowly awhile, and then poised himself stilly upon broad, faintly quivering wings, silent and steady in aim, silent and steady in his arrowy swoop from the low-domed sky. Whether the prey was fascinated by the terror it saw hovering above in ever-narrowing rings, or whether it was drowsing in fancied security, unconscious of the swooping death, Marlowe wondered, when the hawk's plumb descent into the long grass told that the quarry was struck.

Here, in the centre of the heath, stood an assemblage of purply-gray, lichen-broidered stones, roughly ranged, roughly shaped, as if by the sport of some infant giant. The rude, blunt summits of these stones, gray against the darker gray sky, emphasized the desolation by thus re-calling the long-dead creed of a half-for-gotten race, that infant giant who had in sooth flung those grim toys on the heath so many centuries ago in its early blind groping after faith and knowledge, after

the will of the Unseen and the movements of stars, those seen forces seemingly
as inscrutable as the Unseen. Ages and
ages ago both Druids, with their mysterious lore and grim worship, and those
who trembled before them, had vanished,
engulfed in the blackness of time, buried
in the dust of centuries. But neither
dust of dead ages nor darkness of past
time could hide the great stones reared for
dark rites by long-dead hands ; weathered
by the winter storms and baked by the
summer suns of a thousand years, they
still stood solid and intact as at first.
Dust of dust, the hearts whose faith they
embodied may since have passed through
many cycles of being, through the clod
and the blossom that starred it, the fruit
and the bird that pecked it, the stag and
the hunter who wound its death-note on his
long-silenced horn. Yet those mysterious
stones stood.

And not less still than those grim,
time-defying monoliths, the still landscape

boding storm, or the living creatures of the heath, hushed in terror of the hovering hawk, was the figure reclined at the foot of a mænhir, still, as if lost in meditation, still in body as mind, unthinking whether some grim fate were poised hawkwise above the level champaign of his life, or some dark storm of sorrow brewing on its calm horizon. His knapsack lay beside him in the tussocky grass ; the dust of road and forest was on his feet ; his glance rested tranquilly on the landscape, spreading in undulating sweeps of wood and heath, intersected by glen and river, to the sea. Thence, distant as it was, the low, hoarse, continuous roar of the ground-swell was faintly borne to his ears.

Some fir-tree tops feathered towards the open elevated heath, motionless beneath the low, purplish sky, their sealike music hushed in their dark boughs, adding the vague charm of old romance to the magic and mystery of nature. Some-

where beneath those firs did the fabled
fountain of Belenton sparkle, beside the
charmed waters of which the knight
Pontus watched his arms? Or was the
mystic sword hidden in some enchanted
dell in the shade? Local traditions each
contradicted the other; asking the country
folk was of no avail. It was pleasant to
lie in the mysterious stillness of that
neutral-tinted day, when the air was
neither warm nor cold and the autumn-
like peace of the spring day was growing
and growing, and think of what might be
hidden in the heart of the woods, or over
there in the feudal castle with pointed
turrets by the sea.

It was the forest of Broceliande or
Brécheliante, in legend-haunted Brittany,
where, long after the Druids who reared
those dolmens and mænhirs had vanished,
moved the heroes of Arthurian romance.
Romance? The woods gloomed with it,
the air breathed of it, the heath flowers
whispered old tales and murmured magic

spells in the silence ; nothing seemed real, nothing belonged to the prosaic life of to-day, all was poetic dreamland. Somewhere in the heart of the forest lay Merlin, shrouded by his white beard of secular growth, his knowledge useless, his enchantments vain, fast bound through all the centuries by the potency of his own spells. Great and sage wizard to give his magic wand to a false woman ! Did Merlin muse upon Vivien's treachery as he lay there impotent, revolving deeper and deeper spells while the ages rolled by ? Wise Merlin, whose magic could build beautiful halls and strong towers, could bend great kings and mighty warriors to his will, wise old man, outwitted by a slight woman, a mere toy !

Here the knight Tristram hunted, and here under the forest shade he lay in his sorrow, pining for Iseult of Ireland, she who had drunk of the enchanted cup with him. Doubtless his face had often been turned seaward, and his longing thoughts

had overleapt that gray channel whose
waves broke against King Mark's Castle
in Cornwall, where Irish Iseult's youth
was wasting in vain regret. Yonder by
the seashore the younger Iseult, the un-
loved, used to pace under the shining
hollies and mourn her lost Tristram, never
truly hers. Everywhere, as far as eye
could see, extended the site of the ancient
forest of Broceliande, bounded on the
north by the gray sea now hoarsely
threatening in the distance.

The day was passing ; this pleasant
quiescence must be broken. Marlowe
rose, strapped on his knapsack, and
fared forwards over the brown heather
and dry tussocks, aimless and lost in
dreams, till he reached a wood which
must be penetrated or skirted. This was
painful ; it forced him to a decision, in-
terrupting the current of placid reverie.

The path through the wood led south,
away from the sea ; skirting the wood, you
went seawards.

Is it fate or is it will that moves us in critical but apparently trivial moments? Marlowe had no will in the matter—landwards or seawards it was the same to him; he would not have cared one jot but for the effort he had to make in deciding. Time was nothing to him; months lay before him in which he would have no other care than to wander as he listed, no object but to divert his mind and restore the mental balance lost by over-study and the hurry of too full a life. He had passed the first stage of recovery, the totally inert, and had reached the passively receptive, that blissful interlude which is a second and sweeter childhood; all he wanted was to receive new impressions and dream in peace, unvexed by moral considerations or active thought.

So he stood irresolute, gazing at the sea, which, darkening under the darkening sky, was now a deep indigo.

Some gulls sailed above him landwards, their strong curved wings white against

the dark cloud-canopy, their flight level
and swift. It mattered so little which
way he went that it was not worth while
to make the effort of deciding. And yet
one cannot walk across a room without
some exertion of will, therefore he remained still as a stone, and the old, old
Sphinx's riddle of Fate and Will broke in
upon his dreams of old romance. Should
he shut his eyes and go blindly whither
Chance or Fate led him? Why, then
there would still be an act of choice,
because even with shut eyes he would
remember that this way led through the
wood, landwards, and that, by the wood,
seawards. One can do nothing without
some faint volition. Toss up? That
would be an appeal to Fate or Chance.
Does the Power that poises the planet
and gives its long curve to the swallow's
wing work here unobserved in such
matters, where neither instinct, reason,
nor sense move the springs of will?

Storm was coming up rapidly; this

expectant stillness is the precursor of
tempest.   Was that a cry?   Faint and
distant, a low, inexpressibly mournful,
long-drawn, shuddering wail, or rather
moan, passing into a sigh, shivered past
and died away, like the spirit of one of
those fabled knights of old, moaning by in
the desolation, where once was such life
and stir of noble deeds.   Was it Merlin
bewailing his doting folly and the lost
magic of his wand?   Or was it—yes, it
must be, the Genver, sometimes heard
over there in Cornwall, the English
Brittany, as full of legends and saints as
the French—the Genver which is known
to be the soul of Queen Guinevere calling
vainly for ever upon Arthur, as the
Cornish chough is known to utter the cry
of King Arthur's spirit in its pain.   Certainly it was the Genver, the herald of
storm, heard but once in many years,
and that only by the privileged.

Metaphysical subtleties vanished in the
interest kindled by this weird and unac-

countable sound, and Marlowe, lost in
speculating upon the kindred superstitions
of the kindred peninsulas, each dashed
by Atlantic · rollers and separated by
the Channel, fared unconsciously onwards,
dreaming and blind, taking the seaward
path.

Over by the sea, clustered about the
feudal towers, were roofs, blue columns of
smoke, and trees ; there would be shelter
for the night. The shrouded sun was
now near its setting ; massive clouds, piled
before it, were breaking into fiery pillars
and bastions ridged with angry flame; long
rays of stormy yellow flashed out from
the fissures, dyeing the western turrets,
yonder steeple, till now inconspicuous,
those gray dolmens, the budding woods
and the heaths starred with yellow broom,
and kindling the holly thicket into innumerable sparkles. Then on a sudden
the straight smoke-columns were twisted
into spirals and dashed hither and thither,
white horses foamed upon the indigo sea,

the hoarse boom of the breakers deepened and mixed with the roaring ground-swell, the woods shuddered and crashed their branches together, last year's dead red leaves eddied up from the ground and flew out from sheltered boughs on which they still clung, dancing and whirling in the joy of coming storm.

He bent his head cheerfully to the blast, and stepped quickly on, in that mood in which everything pleases, stillness or motion, tempest or sunshine, and even calamity only stirs the blood to a swifter flow. The lusty storm, springing exultantly out of the Atlantic and rioting over land and sea, was as welcome as the dreamy charm of the lonely heath, its salt breath was inspiriting, its tumults and chill gave a zest to the fireside shelter to come.

There was on Cecil's face the absence of historic trace peculiar to youth, the blankness of an unwritten page, together with that other youthful expression of

restrained, yet eager, curiosity and unconscious desire, the marks of a fresh
nature and unawakened passions. But a
young, though not briefless, barrister,
who has seen many curious and not
generally known phases of life, who
dabbles in literature, dallies with politics,
reads with wet towels round his head in
the small hours, when not dancing, fancies
he admires many women and is ill-treated
by one, and finally breaks down and is
advised to take months of rest, thinks
himself old.

Being crossed in love is misery with a
difference, especially when, as in this case,
the misery finds vent in verse. Yet Cecil
Marlowe regarded himself as a man who
had seen affliction, and finally renounced
all entanglements with the fair sex in consequence. But his appetite was good,
he was deeply interested in everything
he saw, and slept at night like the seven
of Ephesus.

The stormy yellow flare had died away,

dusk was now closing in under the wings of rising storm, primroses had taken on the mysterious, meditative look that comes at dewfall, when, above the sound of cracking woods, piping winds, and booming sea, there arose a thin but clear stream of singing from a little glen through which a hidden brook wandered. He stopped to listen; it was a weird, sweet melody, sung in an unknown tongue, and singularly fascinating. Evidently the song of a river-spirit, perhaps the water-fairy, that Celtic Lorelei, the Corregan, whose mystic melody draws the listener with irresistible longing to his death.

Marlowe instantly plunged down into the glen towards the fairy singing—down till the sound of the gurgling water made a burden to the Corregan's song; thus the spell-drawn listener always follows the magic music. Soon he must see the shining golden hair and the baleful light of fairy eyes. But the song stopped abruptly, and there, in mid-stream, the water flowing over her pretty bare feet, stood the Corregan, only a black-haired peasant girl, looking up from startled blue eyes, the common heritage of Irish and Breton Celt.

She was poised lightly on the submerged stepping-stones, with the proud and graceful carriage that comes of bearing burdens on the head. One hand was raised to steady her faggot of dry heath in springing from stone to stone, in the other she carried a sickle; her dress was the trim garb of the district, the skirts kilted high for the passage, showing well-made limbs gleaming in the dusk; the snow-white Breton cap-wings flapped in the wind upon her wholesome face; a bunch of fresh primroses was fastened in her bodice. A picture full of charm.

Though poised in the act of flight, she did not fly, but stood at gaze, her face turned over her shoulder as if fascinated by terror, until Marlowe reached the edge of the stream and wished her

' Good-evening,' and asked the way to the nearest inn.

There was no inn near, she replied, the red blush gradually dying from her face, and the startled fawn-gaze from her eyes ; no, nor any tavern. Shelter for the night? There was the whole village of St. Brileuc. Being now re-assured, she smiled, and sprang to the opposite bank, beckoning to him to follow her, which he did, slipping on the mossy stones, to which her bare feet had easily clung under the water. Had he seen the château by the sea? That was St. Brileuc, she said, in broken French, with a strong country accent.

Followed by Marlowe, she climbed up the little glen, through which the stream babbled down to the sea, talking with the unaffected ease of the French peasant, her feet pressing a mosaic of flower and turf, her face whipped by her broad cap-wings, and thus alternately concealed and re-vealed. They walked on till they reached a pasture grazed by cows, Marlowe wondering when the fairy would melt into another shape or resume her magic song, while the storm grew and the roar of the sea deepened. Presently a man was seen approaching them.

'This is my father, Michel Kérouac,' the Corregan said. Then she explained Marlowe's situation to the strong, square-built Breton, who was leading a small cow, which looked on the stranger with wondering eyes.

So the fairy faded into simple, harmless Renée Kérouac, who lived with her father and mother, Michel and Suzanne Kérouac, in the ruins of the feudal castle.

Père Michel readily agreed to take the belated and storm-driven traveller in for the night, now rapidly closing in upon them, taking care to make good and tangible terms first—no easy matter, considering his broken Breton French and Marlowe's literary book French.

In the midst of all this stammering and

gesticulating, misunderstanding and confusion of tongues, the sound of a bell trembled
through the thunder of the rough sea
and roaring wind.   At this sound Kérouac
stopped short, took off his broad felt hat,
and dropped on his knees where he stood,
the cow's rope thrown over his arm, his
hands busy with a rosary which suddenly
appeared in them.   Down went Renée's
bundle of heath and sickle at the same
signal, and she, too, knelt just where she
stood, her head bent and her face shrouded
by the flapping cap, a rosary appearing
with the same mysterious suddenness in
her hands.   The storm wind roared over
the two bent heads, shaking the father's
long hair and flapping the daughter's
cap; heavy rain-drops fell; the cow stood
patiently chewing the cud, her fur ruffled
by the wind and her head bent from it.
Marlowe, moved by the picture, and wondering at this singular combination of
piety with so keen a love of gain in the
worthy man before him, uncovered his

own thick-curled head to the wind and
rain until the rite was done and his new
friends hurried with him and their four-
footed companion to the shelter of the
ruined castle, now a peasant's home.

CHAPTER II.

THE castle was built on a broad plateau on the top of a cliff beetling over the sea; the outworks had been either destroyed or suffered to fall into ruins; the drawbridge was gone, the dry moat partially filled up. The shells of two turrets, united by a battlemented curtain, remained intact, their solid masonry defying not only time, weather, war and democratic rule, which last decreed its destruction lest it should become a stronghold for Chouans, but the violence of marauding peasants, always ready to seize on it for building materials.

A flight of uneven stone steps, flanked

by a broken balustrade and garnished by pots of flowers and shrubs, led to the central entrance between the turrets ; the door of this opened immediately into a fair-sized hall, floored with stone and weather-tight. The bare stone walls, once hung with arras, and even now showing a few broken carved bosses and scutcheons, were faintly seen near the hearth in the glow of the fire ; the farther part of the hall was lost in thick shadow.

Two bed-places with sliding oak panels in the walls, some oaken presses, a table, some benches, and rough cooking and eating vessels, made nearly all the furniture ; this was grouped about the hearth, in the glow of which an elderly woman sat spinning. Two sturdy, long-haired youths were mending nets, one singing in a low monotonous, melancholy recitative, to which the other contributed a sort of antiphon at intervals. When the heavy door creaked open to admit Michel, Renée

and the stranger, the low chant and the
hum of the wheel were drowned in the
thunder of surf on the shore and the war
of winds round the turrets, but when
Père Michel shut and fastened the door
again, mingled agreeably with hushed
sounds of storm.

> 'Shall it be my robe of blue,
>   Or my gown of scarlet hue ?' *

sang Raoul.

> 'Garments of black, my daughter dear,
>   It is now the manner to wear,'

his brother Gabriel was chanting, when
the song stopped at sight of the stranger.

'An English painter, storm-driven, to
pass the night and perhaps some weeks,
mother,' Kérouac announced, as Cecil
stepped into the warm hearth-glow, the
flames dancing in his large dark eyes and
thick-waved hair.

Mère Suzanne's wheel stopped ; she
rose, a gaunt labour-bowed figure, with
hard brown hands and lined brown face,
on which the fine white cap-wings made

* Archbishop Trench's translation.

weird shadows, and said something by way of welcome, signing him to a seat by the fire. The long-haired lads scowled as they made way by the hearth and uttered a surly greeting, while the guest, with the smile of a man who knows how to make sure of a welcome anywhere, stammered out such salutations as he could muster, and took his place with an agreeably fatigued and contented air. This was a pleasant dream in which he lost past and future and his own personality.

The table was soon spread with country fare—galette of buckwheat, fish fresh caught, and buttermilk. Mère Suzanne even cast a hesitating eye on the hams hanging in the large chimney, but was quickly frowned down by the judicious Michel. Foolish forks and troublesome tablecloth were alike eschewed in this simple household, but the board shone bright and clean ; it had a hollow scooped in its centre for the family soup, into which each dipped his own wooden spoon in turn. Cecil was soon enlightened as to the number of purposes to which wooden spoons can be applied, and marvelled that mankind in general should toil to make, labour to buy and keep clean, and fret to be without, that numerous and complicated arrangement of silver, glass, china and napery seen on the tables of the sophisticated. He was hungry, the fare was satisfying, he had the lark's happy knack of looking neither before nor after, and at once became one of that household, and felt as if he had never lived elsewhere.

After supper old cider was produced ; they sat round the spacious hearth, listening to the muffled thunder of storm and sea, and talking in broken French cked out with Celtic, of fairies and enchantments, sea tempests and wasting wars, while the women span, Renée silent by her mother's side, her star-like eyes dilating at thrilling adventure and weird legend.

Cecil's imagination played freely about these things ; his eyes, often too intense of gaze, grew soft with dream and fancy, his mind, empty of all else, lay open to a passive reception of fairy- and folk-lore, legend and song ; it was very restful.

Presently his host led him from the hall along a dark stone passage, where the thick solid walls subdued the shrieking and roaring storm to a low slumbrous murmur, thence up a winding stone stair to a turret chamber, from the deep embrasured windows of which they caught in the darkness the ghostly glimmer of churning surf-sheet and rolling wave-crest. Moon and stars were hidden, but the dark waste of waters was now and again illumined by a flash of lightning.

'It was here that the Sieur de Brigny——' Michel began, but Cecil was too drowsy to be curious even about the ghostly occupants of the turret chamber, and was soon lying in sweet-smelling homespun, lulled by the ceaseless boom of

breakers and roar of winds in a deep
sleep till morning.

The wind howled through the turrets
above, lashing itself madly round tower
and battlement, shrieking as if in impotent effort to shake the thick stone
that had resisted so much storm and
violence; it wailed along corridors and
rioted through ruins; it lifted the great
sea-ridges in its unseen grasp and flung
them in white raging masses on the rocky
shore; it ploughed dark furrows along
the face of the gray sea and made weird
music among the trees, but all its fury
failed to rouse the sleepers in the ruined
castle.   Presently the dark-blue heaven
was swept bare and made to reveal its
shining treasure of stars; the rain rushed
on and on till it was spent in the fury of
the wind, which raved its last and fell.

Then the morning leapt brightly from
behind the eastern hills, and stained the
quieting foam-crests of the gray sea purest
rose.   The time-worn turrets blushed in

the rose light; bleak heaths studded with
sparkling hollies were dyed in it; the
channel waves broke and tumbled in the
redness, like joyous young creatures at
play; the white cliffs of England glowed
in it and her gray downs brightened;
the canopy of London mist was steeped
in it, and rolled slowly away in heavy
crimson folds, changing to opal, till by
degrees the vast city stood, but for the
light smoke-veil, bare in its ugliness and
squalor, its splendour and luxury, to the
brilliant May-day sunshine. Budding
lindens and elms in parks and gardens
were jewelled with freshest green, spring-
flowers glowed in windows and balconies;
the grime and ugliness of the great grim
town was half masked by all this bravery
of sunlight and greenery.

Even the smoke-stained dreariness of
those avenues of monotonous porticoed
houses, drab and dismal, running south-
ward from Hyde Park, almost forgot itself
in the glow of the fresh spring morning;

the very tulips, deutzias, and hyacinths on the porticos and miniature balconies forgot that they were exiles, and ignored the dust and smut on their leaves as the glory of the morning grew on towards noon, passed it and still deepened.

Inside one of these flower-adorned houses some children were gathered in the hall, looking with delighted interest up the staircase to the wide landing.

'Oh my!' cried the tallest of the group, which had just broken loose from school-room and nursery, 'isn't our Cyn a howling swell?'

At this a door opposite the children opened, and a middle-aged gentleman of prim and precise deportment appeared. He, too, gazed with an air of approving patronage up the staircase, down which came a faded lady, shawled, and with the dowdy aspect of a chronic invalid, just as the loud thunder of a knocker plied by the practised hand of a footman arose. The door being opened, the figure of a soldierly-looking old gentleman carrying a bouquet and followed by a younger man appeared. They, too, after a word with the faded lady and her precise husband, joined in the general gaze up the staircase, the gazers by this time being augmented by servants and other members of the family peeping from various nooks and points of vantage. The baby danced and crowed in the nurse's arms; two little children, restrained by the hands of a grave governess, cried ' Oh !' and the cynosure of all eyes, a young lady in court dress, with a serious, sweet face, sailed slowly down the stairs with a cordial ' How do you do, General Marlowe? How do you do, Captain Marlowe? And oh, mamma! pray tell me am I carrying my tail properly?'

> ' " Pussy cat, pussy cat, where have oo been ?
> Up to London to see the Creen," '

warbled a boy voice; and a four-year-old girl whimpered; ' P'ease let me have on my party fock, and go and see the Keen, too !'

'Stand back, children,' said Mrs. Forde-Cusacke ; 'and, remember, no one is on any account to kiss Cynthia.'

'A most tantalizing order,' murmured the General ; 'you should not put such things into people's heads.'

'I will kiss you all round when I come home, if you are good,' said Cynthia in her serious way, meaning the children.

'We will indeed be good,' murmured the General, to the discomposure of his son.

'I had no idea,' said Mr. Forde-Cusacke, in his impenetrable pomposity, 'that Cynthia would carry off feathers and a train so well. Allow me to compliment you on your appearance, my dear.'

'Thank you, papa,' she replied, curt-seying demurely. 'Nurse tells me it is no credit, because fine feathers make fine birds.'

'Nurse is out for once, for all her

wisdom,' said Captain Marlowe. 'No amount of feathers would make a magpie carry his tail like a peacock.'

'Thank you for the comparison. Your bouquet is beyond thanks, General. Has poor dear Lady Susan been waiting all this time?'

'I say, Cyn,' called out the eldest boy, 'don't you get in a funk like that girl——'

'Hush, Marmie!' cried mamma. 'Don't be afraid of stepping on your train in going backwards, Cynnie.'

'Oh, mother! should I be sent to the Tower if I did?' asked Cynthia, taking the General's arm, and giving her bouquet to his son to carry.

'Is this a subject for levity, Miss Brande?' asked the latter. 'History is silent on the fate of such unlucky ladies.'

'So are the newspapers, probably for state reasons,' added the General, handing her into the carriage; 'only one thing is certain, they are never heard of again.'

Cynthia, unlike many ladies on their
way to that Drawing-room, had no cause
to fear the searching blaze of the May
sun ; her slim white throat, fair shoulders,
and fresh, innocent face, were all the
fairer and fresher in the beautiful light,
as young verdure and May flowers
are.

Her court finery seemed as suitable
and as natural to her as her simplest
morning gown ; the soft waving of curling
white plumes subdued the flash of jewels
and sheen of rich rustling stuffs; the flowers
in her hand accorded with the soft bloom
of her face ; shining eyes and silky hair
were set off by the white, uncovered
shoulders. Her light, swift step, accustomed to meadows and country lanes,
steep cliffs, and slippery downs, was properly subdued to a sedate. and measured
pace on the carpeted pavement, to the
wonder of Dick Marlowe, who almost
expected daisies to spring up in her path.
Yet 'little Cynthia,' as her friends still

called the tall, slight, unformed girl, was
scarcely a beauty.

There was a captivating sweetness in
the curves of her lips, but as yet no
strength or decision; her eyes, clear-
shining with wholesome youth, were
neither very well set nor very well
coloured, but people who knew her in-
timately were fascinated by their expression and the unexpected lights they flashed
out at times; their gaze even when
smiling was serious, almost sad, as if looking into a dark and tragic future. Lady
Susan, scanning her charge with critical
yet approving glance, observed this look,
often seen in the portraits of those destined
to sorrow or early death, with pain and
uneasy foreboding, for she loved the girl,
and was superstitious.

The carriage door was shut, the shining
steeds dashed off with a glitter of turning
wheels and a gleam of diamonds and find
raiment, to the admiration of a crowd
of street-boys and nursemaids, and the

quieter interest of the two Marlowes, who
gazed after it till a bend of the street took
it, before they turned back to the Forde-
Cusackes'.

' Fine girl, Dick !' said the elder man,
stepping aside while a servant rolled up
the red cloth.

' Certainly, sir.'

' Fine property, Dick !'

' Quite so.'

' Nice girl, Dick !' continued the General,
emphasizing the adjective.

' Very.'

' Nice manner, eh ?'

' Of course.'

' Good girl, Dick?'

' Very.'

' Good action, h'm ?'

' Precisely,' returned Richard, by this
time once more in the little entrance-hall
with his father.

He knew what the General expected of
him, and he thought it on the whole
rough upon Cynthia thus, as it were, to

snap her up on the threshold of her social
life. In his simple creed it was mean to
make advances to a girl before she came
out and had an opportunity of exercising
some choice.

Mrs. Forde-Cusacke had been unable
to present her daughter in the previous
spring on account of interesting family
events ; and, an event of equal interest
being imminent this year, and the same
kind of thing having gone on for the last
ten years, it had occurred to Mrs. Forde-
Cusacke that Cynthia ran some risk of
not going to St. James's at all if she
waited to present her in person. Therefore Lady Susan Marlowe had undertaken
this very serious duty, and Cynthia would
have been taken ' to see the Keen ' in
March, but for the prolonged illness of
Lady Susan's youngest son.

Cynthia regarded the ceremony with
the dutiful seriousness that characterized
her ; it was, of course, far less serious
than confirmation, though bearing the

same relation to secular matters that did to spiritual. As the carriage rolled through the bustling roads she mused on the new duties her mother told her she would now have to fulfil. But while she mused a light came to her, and the solemnity of those duties vanished.

'Why, Cynthia,' Lady Susan said caressingly, ' what a grave face for this bright day ! One might think you a judge going to open assizes.'

'Of course,' she returned, the gravity vanishing, 'I see now why judges are so gorgeously dressed ; fine clothes make one thoughtful.'

'What thoughts does your finery inspire, dear child ?'

'I suppose,' Cynthia continued, 'it is being unused to full dress in the morning. But I can't forget my feathers, dear Lady Susan ; and I can't help wondering why I should be decked out in all this frippery.'

'My dear child ! simply because others are.'

'The children's governess is not. And the girls in those shops, most of them young, many very pretty; and those girls with band-boxes and parcels hurrying along the pavement.'

'Dearest Cynthia, their duties are different; they are not in society.'

'Then why am I? And what does society mean, after all? A round of amusement.'

'A very tiring round,' sighed Lady Susan, who was going to St. James's solely for Cynthia's sake.

'Don't think me ungrateful. But would you rather be bending over wash-tubs, or scrubbing floors, like other—ah! —other people's mothers? And don't you think Maria would rather drive along to St. James's this bright day with the General's lovely flowers than be shut up in the nursery or walking in the square with the children? or Charlotte, who is in the kitchen cooking? Then Jane, scrubbing and dusting, and Hannah

scolded yesterday for wearing smart ear-
rings—and factory girls ?   Why shouldn't
they all wear diamonds ?'

' In the first place there are not enough
diamonds for all,' Lady Susan replied ;
' and if there were, no one would care to
wear diamonds.   You are beginning to
confuse yourself by social problems—
problems not so hard as they seem,
Cynthia.   The adornments of life are not
so unnecessary as you think ; society is
more useful than it seems.   Your place
is among the adornments of life.   It is
not happier than a graver and more useful
lot ; but here your duty lies.'

' Why should my lot be all ornament,
others all labour ?'

' Why is a cabbage a cabbage, and a
rose a rose ?'

' It seems nobler to be a cabbage and
feed some poor and useful labourer——'

' Than to be a rose sung by poets,
given as a love-pledge and treasured for
years.   You will soon find that this

ornamental life of yours has serious duties
enough and to spare.'

Cynthia's eyes were shining with un-
shed tears. She turned them from her
friend and looked at the crowd gathered
before the palace gate, at which they
were now waiting in an unusually long
queue.

What mysteries life holds ! How deeply
this young untried girl longed to raise the
veil from the soul dimly imaged beneath
those commonplace, every-day faces, bent
in derision, depreciation, or utter stolidity
upon the line of carriages freighted with
fine raiment and jewels !

Beneath those rich garments and soft-
flowing plumes were human forms and
human hearts, the hopes of maiden youth,
the cares of matronly maturity and world-
worn age, mean cares and mean ambitions,
much foiled and stifled nobility, some lofty
aspirations and pure aims. Aims, hopes,
ambitions, cares and heroisms—all were
represented in the neutral-tinted crowd

on the pavement as in the jewelled,
bright-hued throng in the carriages. Both
were alike, both human; and though the
silk-clad people on the whole possessed
more knowledge and more inherited intellect than the others, the chief difference
between them consisted in the amount
of soap expended daily upon each.

A pale girl, looking tired and dis-
pirited, was selling flowers on the pavement—she had great pathetic dark eyes,
surpassed by none beneath the ostrich
feathers; a bare-footed grimy boy was
turning wheels with his body—his eyes
were sharp and cunning; some country
cousins were seeing the procession of
courtiers for the first time; street boys
were making free comments on the ladies
compelled to wait before them with that
guileless oblivion of the feelings of others
peculiar to boys and unpolished men;
grown-up roughs were surpassing these
ingenuous youths in their comments; the
impassive British policeman and the im-

perturbable British footman looked on
stolidly and perambulators with screech-
ing occupants got in the way.

Absorbed in this scene, Cynthia
wondered and wondered and wondered
again what kind of picture life showed to
all these eyes, why so many went ragged,
shabby and dingy, while so few were
plumed and richly dressed. But Lady
Susan had eyes only for Cynthia, who sat
nearest the pavement, and whose absorbed
and thoughtful face was turned in half-
profile from her.

'Dear child! if she were my very own I
could not care more for her,' the elder
lady mused ; and yet she did not wish her
to marry her son Richard.

CHAPTER III.

ST. JAMES'S PALACE.

CYNTHIA continued to perplex herself with unanswerable problems and vague speculations, while her friend, as absorbed as she, went on thinking of Cynthia and forecasting her future, partly on the insufficient data of the undeveloped and faulty character she had studied in this young creature of late, and partly on her circumstances and promise of beauty. Lady Susan had made some plaintive allusions to the tyrannous necessity of appearing in a low-necked gown in the morning. Yet she was not to be pitied : an artist would have preferred the grand moulding of her shoulders and arms to

Cynthia's indefinite outlines. This lady
had been very beautiful in youth, and,
though now long past the meridian of
life, she showed no trace of age, unless
it were its mellowing, and the tolerant
gentleness that can only come with years.
Her eyes sparkled with the fire of intellect
and glowed with the warmth of a good
heart, and she possessed other unfading
charms. To her youngest and favourite
son she was the most beautiful woman
he had ever seen. Their relationship was
an ideal one, as Cynthia knew, and, with
a sudden blush for the egoism which had
brought nothing but her own personal
perplexities into their half-hour's conversation, she turned from the motley crowd
in the spring sunshine to the beautiful
face looking so kindly upon her, and asked
if Lady Susan had heard from her son
Cecil.

The older face was at once irradiated,
the beautiful eyes softened. She had but
just received one of the long journal-

letters with which Cecil dotted his route, and, knowing it would be a crowded Drawing-room, she had brought it with her, thinking it might beguile the tedium of waiting.

'A capital thought! Your son is such a delightful correspondent,' replied Cynthia, who always said the right thing.

Cecil Marlowe's letter was a prospective infliction to her, and, while listening civilly to her friend's reading, her serious thoughts flowed on in an under-current. She began to understand why so many people in old times, like the beautiful young bride killed at her own marriage-feast, had worn hair-cloth beneath their raiment of cloth of gold and silver tissues.

'I think he *is* rather a good correspondent,' Lady Susan replied, with a wistful bashfulness that would have been rather touching to one ten years older than Cynthia. 'He is observant and imaginative, and his pen flows gracefully.'

'A poet, too. I think you saw the review of his "Daffodil Songs"?'

'Yes; clever people always begin with verse, Cynthia, but only foolish ones go on. Verse is a kind of mental measles : one is glad when it comes well out and is over.'

'I shall always admire your son's measles, and look for another attack'— an exact reflection of Lady Susan's own secret thoughts ; she would have liked to kiss Cynthia for saying it. 'In the meantime, I hope his prosaic ailments are gone, and he is enjoying his travel.'

'He is thoroughly in love with Brittany and his own freedom. "I don't in the least know how I got here," he writes ; "some pleasant spring air drifted me, perhaps. Brittany is all historic association, poetry, legend, romance. It is impossible to live the prose of everyday life in these haunted regions ; I live and move in an enchanting dream."'

'Do you think——' began Cynthia.

'Well, dear ? One might think you

were about to charge a jury, from your face.'

Cynthia laughed and blushed.

'I was only wondering if it were a good plan to live in dreams,' she replied.

'Bad for the morals, Cynnie, as a rule. But relaxation is just what the poor boy wants now—a purely animal life. Let me see—where was I? Oh! "How strange that Chateaubriand, born at St. Malo, bred in the haunted forest of Broceliande, where every stick and stone speaks of romance and history, should have gone to the silent and desolate American forests for inspiration! Inspiration is best found at home, Goethe says. It was the tendency of Chateaubriand's time—a violent breaking away from the old, however lovely—an eager thirst for the new, however blank and featureless.—My movements are undecided. I may go on into the Basque provinces, and thence down into Moorish Spain, or along the Mediterranean coast to Italy, provided I don't

fall into Merlin's enchanted circle, or hear
the Corregan sing. So think nothing
wrong if I do not write for a few weeks.'

'This must result in more measles,
surely,' Cynthia said, thanking Lady Susan
for the reading. 'How well I seem to
know your son by this time!'

'Did you ever meet him?'

'Not since I was a child. I was in
great awe of Mr. Cecil as a grown man.
I remember meeting him with the General
in the garden at Cottesloe. I made my
first and last approach to a repartee on
that occasion.'

'Dear Cynthia, I have heard some
since. This must have been very fine to
be remembered so long.'

'One's first, Lady Susan, and by accident. He was teasing me. "If a herring
and a half cost three-halfpence, how many
would you get for a shilling?" he asked.
I said, "None, because I would never buy
anything so nasty." The General was
hugely delighted at my supposed wit, the

point of which it took me seven years to
see.   Mr. Cecil shook his head and said I
was a fair deception, and I felt that I
must be very clever somehow, though
I couldn't quite see how.   From that
moment, dear Lady Susan, I steadily
grew out of all my frocks, and entertained
the highest opinion of your son's mental
endowments.'

'But why from that moment?'

'Why, because I found that they were
nearly as good as my own.   Besides,
nobody else had ever accused me of
sharpness,' she replied, with an innocent
look.

'Cynthia,' returned Lady Susan, 'you
are a naughty girl.   I would kiss you
if the policeman were not looking.   I
wonder how it is that you and Cecil
always miss seeing each other.'

Here further conversation was prevented by admission to the palace, where
Cynthia's attention was riveted by the
occupants of the other carriages, and

especially by those girls who, like herself, were about to be presented. Daintily nurtured, and for the most part well born, what future lay before them, she pondered—what golden sorrows, jewelled shames and tinselled cares? Did they, too, ponder on the strange inequalities of human lots, and wonder why they went in silks and others in rags?

Their *devoir* accomplished, they returned to the Marlowes' house, where Lady Susan received that afternoon.

Perhaps it was not pure chance that placed a new and very successful photograph of the author of 'Daffodil Songs' and future Lord Chancellor conspicuously on a table near which Cynthia Brande was sitting. A copy of the poems being there also, it was inevitable that she should both turn its pages and look at the writer's face; inevitable, too, that she should think of her friend's especial tenderness for this son, and wonder what qualities called it forth. Lady Susan was an affectionate

wife and mother ; her soldier and sailor
sons, Harry and Dick, nice fellows both,
were very dear to her, but this unknown
Cecil, reputed so clever, known to have
fallen ill from over - activity of mind,
dashing off those charming poems as a
sort of preliminary mental canter, writing
so fully and frequently to his mother, and
in such perfect intellectual accord with
that charming and clever woman, must
surely possess something to justify her
passionate affection.   He must have heart
as well as intellect, refinement and good
principle.   She wondered what he thought
about diamonds, and if he were troubled
because of those who sat in the dust of
life.   After all, delightful as Lady Susan
was, she was only a woman, and perhaps
at her age it was natural that she should
take things too much for granted. Cynthia
was sorry that she had no brother older
than Marmie.   How pleasant it would be
to discuss things of vital interest with
a man friend of one's own age !

She did not know that she was lonely ; but what with the annual advent of a little Forde-Cusacke, and the many claims of those already in existence—not to speak of social duties and the perpetual requirements of Mr. Forde-Cusacke, whose life was an eternal succession of fads and fusses, for each of which he required a perpetual fountain of fresh-springing sympathy, unadulterated by criticism— poor Mrs. Cusacke had scant leisure for her eldest child, the daughter of her youth and romance. On the other hand, Marmaduke Forde-Cusacke, Esq., M.P., had never yet betrayed any interest in anyone's concerns but his own — except, indeed, in those of mankind at large, which he felt bound to favour with his patronage and partial approval. So Cynthia lived in isolation, and could only discuss things in her own heart until the happy time when Lady Susan began to make a companion and friend of her. Anecdotes of Cecil's boyhood were not unknown to Cynthia, and especially the story of his devoted servant, Bob Ryall. Bob, ill-treated by a tipsy tinker, was the spoil of war. Cecil, a stripling in his teens, had fought the big tinker for possession of the boy and won. She liked that story ; her eyes became luminous at the remembrance.

'Very good likeness of Will, is it not?' said Captain Marlowe, coming up.

'Will?' she asked, returning from reverie to reality, with a flush and a sparkle.

'I forgot ; you only know my brother Cecil by his Sunday name.'

'Quite so. He doesn't look like a plain Will,' she replied. 'Have you an every-day name, too?'

'We've all Sunday names ; none of them stick but Will's. My mother tried to keep to them all. The rest of us can't rise above plain Tom, Dick and Harry. Fancy calling me St. Maur. You laugh, Miss Brande, at the bare notion.'

'Why not St. Maur? But Richard
is more manly and well-sounding. And
why should your brother be known by his
most imposing name? It strikes me as
an odd talent.'

'It hangs together with a fellow in an
Oxford reading set, a man who scribbles
verse and stuff, a " learned brother " and
all that sort of thing, you know. The
rest of us haven't an ounce of brains between us, thank the Lord! We take after
the General.'

'Oh, Captain Marlowe, think of the
Fifth Commandment!'

'Well, so I do, only the other way
about. So you managed to escape the
Tower this morning! And you had
nobody to look after you!'

'No,' Cynthia replied, 'we relied on
your faithless brother.'

'He ought to have telegraphed in
time,' Dick added; 'fearful grind for you,
wasn't it? Men are always tumbling
over their swords at Court. I often

wonder there are no more spills from ladies' trains.'

'Ladies are used to be followed. No; beyond ordering the Duke of Oxford—who seems to be a grand Court official, or three-tailed bashaw—to run and call Lady Susan Marlowe's carriage, and *be quick*, under the impression that he was some kind of servant, I don't know that I did anything very dreadful.'

'What happened?'

'He ran. I didn't enjoy the subsequent introduction.'

'No doubt *he* did. He isn't a bad lot. A sort of eight-hundredth cousin of my mother's. Shall I get you an ice?'

Cynthia knew that conversation with Dick could never rise above this level. Yet Dick was like his mother, with just such fine eyes, but they were blue instead of black.

Away south in Brittany that bright afternoon, Cecil Marlowe was sitting in the

sun under a blossomed apple-tree, within
sound of the quieted sea, pen in hand.

' I wish you were here,' he wrote, after
a description of St. Brileuc ; ' it is like
living a century back, so many obsolete
customs linger on. No papers, no books,
no bothers. No one has ever heard anything of the present ; they are still
trying to catch up with the past at a
snail's gallop. I shall stay a week or
two longer and collect songs and legends,
a lodger in that enchanted turret-chamber
which you would love.—I have heard
and seen the Corregan and yet live.
She withheld the usual proposals, no
doubt detecting the budding old bachelor
in me. She turned out to be a harmless
peasant girl, not exactly handsome, but
picturesque, and with something of the
half-childish, half-savage grace of her
class. You would instantly have sketched
her, if you had come upon her singing on
the stepping-stones in the stream at dusk.
My daughters (old bachelors always have

daughters) shall carry things on their
heads to develop their figures.—By the
way, how does Dick's courtship speed?
Harry said he was hopelessly gone on
your pet girl-friend. It cuts me to the
heart to see the women doing hard
field work. Mère Suzanne turns out
to be quite young, and is a regular old
hag to look at. Even the beautiful
Breton eyes are bleared. The poor
Corregan's will soon fade, I suppose.
Such eyes ! All the poetry and romance,
the endurance, the weird witchery and
superstition of the race seem to look out
upon you through long, long centuries
from their blue deeps. " Me the fairy
has looked to death," says the ballad of
the Corregan, and no wonder. She has
a sweetheart—the peasant Corregan—he
looks at her as if she were a goddess now;
but he will make her work in his fields
and drudge in his house when he marries
her. She, who pretends to scorn him
now, will make no secret of worshipping

him then.   I don't like that slavishness
in women—another old bachelor's trait.
But when I think of the uses to which
men put women in this beast of a
world, I declare I would as soon be a
Barbary ape as a man.   You would find
Raoul and Gabriel Kérouac irresistible for
models.—The General must bring you
near this place in the autumn.   He could
bathe and knock about pleasantly for a
week or two.   Glad to hear that little
Cynthia Brande has grown so companionable for you.   I dug for two hours in the
garden this morning, and dined (at noon)
on mackerel fresh from the sea.   One can
bathe here in Father Adam's coat.   What
does hearing the Genver portend ?'

Some little time passed without a line
from Cecil.   The next letter was brief,
speaking of the tranquil monotony and
healthful stupidity of a purely animal
existence, ruinous to letter-writing.   Then
followed a longer silence, which, though it
disappointed, did not disquiet Lady Susan.

Days sped rapidly at St. Brileuc; leaves unfolded as if by magic, the glory of the year grew apace, life was as a pleasant dream, the past as if it had not been, the future as if it would not be ; only the golden present was there, and sunshine was sweet.   Cecil's mind, bruised and strained by his strenuous life, had drifted into a neutral-tinted valley of rest, which was dim and unreal, and peopled by shades, like the vague, still pleasaunce of Elysian fields, or that even stiller valley of Avilion, in which King Arthur rested after his grievous wound in the last weird battle.

Ostensibly there to sketch, Cecil lived the simple life of his hosts, going afield with them on land or a-fishing in the sea, chatting with them and their companions on Sundays and holidays, sometimes lending a hand at their labours, sometimes taking the boat and going off by himself for a day, sometimes going inland in search of Druidic remains and antiquities.   The turret-chamber was a stronghold to resort to when he wished to be alone, which was seldom. He liked better to join the family circle round the hearth-fire in the hall, when the evenings were chill, or in the pale warm twilights and moonlit nights to sit outside on the small terrace by the flight of stone steps. Then it was that old ballads were droned, old tales told, and country customs and superstitions discussed, as they never had been before ; for peasants never describe themselves, and do not discuss things which are as natural and obvious to them as the shining of the sun and stars. But Cecil Marlowe, trained to draw information from uneducated minds, already understood how, by subtle and well-directed questions, to educe valuable facts and shatter unstable theories, a knowledge which subsequently made him so skilful in examining and cross-examining witnesses. Besides, he knew how to suppress himself and suggest trains of thought that made people forget his presence and reveal their mental stores in anecdote, reminiscence or half-unconscious soliloquy.

This was especially the case with the women, whose minds were more plastic and tongues readier than those of the men, and who were often at home, sitting by the hearth or at the open door spinning, while the men were away. He was very sorry for these hard-worked, patient women, with their deeper needs and finer organizations added to their physical weakness and emotional dependence. Renée was the object of his more compassionate interest, because he saw by a hundred tokens that her heart had put forth its spring blossoming, and her life of toil and care was brightened by the one gleam of romance which love sheds on such. And Hoël Calloc, her reputed sweetheart, was a rough, coarse fellow, low-browed, with a fierce animal eye and heavy jaw. Cecil did not like Hoël, and Hoël disliked 'that fine Englishman.'

CHAPTER IV.

A NIGHT ON THE ROCKS.

THOUGH Love levels ranks, he rarely does it without disaster—to the woman. Did not the Lady of Burleigh die of an affectionate husband's splendour? Semele was slain by the first glimpse of her lover's glory; worse things happened to that unfortunate Vestal, whose semi-divine offspring were thrown into the Tiber to be rescued by a wolf's compassion. Syrinx and Daphne only escaped the pursuit of divine adorers by over-stepping the bounds of humanity and living faintly on in the cold tissues of reed and laurel by favour of a woman god. In these cases the man always gets the

best of it.   For Diana, far from harming
her loved shepherd, raised Endymion to
her own silver courts, and Aurora con-
ferred immortality upon Tithonus.   But
if the god-like lover is only a prince,
peer, or gentleman, and the woman the
daughter of one whose loftiest title is
plain man, her disaster is even deeper.

The world of St. Brileuc saw that the
mysterious stranger, who, like an old
Greek god in disguise, had come among
them from Heaven knew where, if ostensibly from a land of fog and barbarians
beyond the sea, perceived the beauty of
Michel Kérouac's daughter, nor was this
quite unsuspected by Renée herself.
Cecil would often say to her, ' Renée, are
you not very tired ?' or, ' That is hard
work for a woman,' and more frequently
still he would carry some burden, or
do a piece of field work for her.   Then
her eyes would deepen as she looked
with astonishment, mingled with pleasure,
into the foreign artist's searching dark

eyes, and Cecil would wonder how it was that the women of her class are so much more interesting than the men, and his heart would ache with pity to think of the life that lay before her.

'Why should you do my work?' she asked haughtily, as if it were a stigma on her to be thought too feeble for it, one day when he found her bending over a piece of fresh-turned ground that she was manuring with *goëmon*, or sea-wrack, gathered from the bouldered shore, and tried to take the fork from her hands.

'Think how much you do for me,' he replied, getting possession of the fork, while she straightened her aching back and took out the knitting which served to fill up pauses when the busy hands were not otherwise occupied—when, for instance, she was going to market with her jar of butter poised on her head. 'Thanks to you, Renée, I can say many things in Breton. And I want you to do something more, with your mother's leave. I want you to let me paint you.'

'Me ! What, like the picture you made of the sea, with Raoul and Gabriel in the boat ? Then I must wear my buckled shoes and the clothes I wore at the Pardon. No, no, it cannot be,' she added, her pride suddenly taking fire.

'But why not ?' Michel Kérouac said afterwards to his wife. 'To make pictures is his trade. A cat may look at a king. If the Englishman may look at our girl, why not paint her, as he did the cow ?'

So Renée was painted, with the startled gaze in her deep eyes and the bundle of heather on her head, barefoot on the mossy stepping-stones as he had first seen her, and they were all pleased that he should paint a mænhir topped by a crucifix in the background. That was good against evil spirits and bad luck.

The sittings took place of an evening in front of the ruined château, in the presence of Mère Suzanne, and did not prevent the daughter from plying her distaff, and her mother both tongue and wheel. Neighbours strolled in and watched progress with audible comments, mostly unintelligible to the painter, in one of the numerous country dialects. Renée, half defiant, half bashful, kept her strained position, standing on the lowest step with the upward gaze required, and the bundle of heather, which Cecil took care should be light, on her head, until she became pale with a fatigue she denied. Did they think her so weak? How could she be tired of standing still and doing nothing? She was no child; she could do this and that with any girl in the country. Hoël's criticisms on this piece of art were acrid.

It was during these sittings that Marlowe met with the accident that so nearly cost him his life. They were at a wedding —Renée, Gabriel, Raoul, and Marlowe, the latter an incongruous figure in his plain touring suit and felt hat among the

gay peasants in their various costumes;
the men with long hair, broad-leaved hats
adorned with buckles and streamers, and
some (those of Hoël's parish) with several
jackets worn one over the other, and em-
broidered in gay colours, with full velvet
knickerbockers and bright-buckled shoes;
the women in every variety of white cap
and apron, with bodices of bright rich
stuffs, short, much-trimmed dark skirts,
and buckled shoes instead of workaday
sabots.   The bride literally blazed in
raiment of cloth of gold and silver tissue,
with bejewelled head-gear; the bridegroom
glittered, and his long black curls shone in
the sunshine. Tables were spread beneath
trees in the first freshness of full leaf,
where on the grass, within sound of the
sea beating gently on the granite-bouldered
shore, the dancing took place.

Marlowe was enchanted with the brilliance and simple gaiety of the sight as he
sat in the shade with the elders, the
women knitting or spinning, and looked

on at the gavotte, a long string of couples coiling and uncoiling itself round the head couple like a large and many-coloured ribbon, to the country music, which had the Celtic melancholy even in its mirth.

While thus occupied, the magnetism of an intense gaze made him look up and meet the fierce blaze of Hoël Calloc's glowing black eyes. Calloc was not dancing—a circumstance that made Marlowe look round in search of Renée, who also was not among the dancers. She was sitting close by on the grass, within earshot.

Thereupon, to the fierce wrath of Hoël Calloc, whose eyes blazed like a hungry tiger's, he left his place and let himself down on the grass by the reluctant damsel's side.

'What is all this about?' he asked, diverted by the notion of arranging a lovers' quarrel. 'Why don't you dance? Look at poor Calloc sulking and kicking his heels for want of a partner. May I

not tell him he is forgiven ?   I am sure
he is penitent.'

'That Calloc !' cried Renée scornfully,
her cheeks crimson with fury ; 'that
animal !   What have I to do with him ?
I would rather dance with a pig !'

'Come now, come! You know the poor
fellow is desperately in love——'

'Love indeed !   Is it love to follow a
poor girl about everywhere with his
devilries ?   Oh, I hate him ! I hate him !
I would rather touch a toad !   He knows
it.   I never encouraged him—never !'

Cecil laughed, and assured her that
hate made a capital beginning, and Renée's
anger and agitation grew with his half-
mischievous proposals to negotiate in the
matter.

'And I *fear* him,' she added beneath
her breath.

'What, you, who fear nothing—turkey-
cocks, mad bulls, squalls at sea ?   *You*
fear ?'

'Ah, monsieur,' she panted, 'but I fear

this man. He has sold himself to the devil ; his master protects him. Oh, he is strong ! Some say he is a *loup-garou.*'

' There are no *loups-garous*, my dear child, and the devil would not give a bad sou for his soul. But never mind ; Calloc shan't bother you. I'll see to that—for to-night at least.'

He looked so kindly at Renée as he said this, reclined on one elbow by her side, and she blushed so pleasurably and looked so happy, that the unlucky Calloc swore his very greatest oath, and his eyes rolled till nothing but the whites were visible.

Cecil was as good as his word, and successfully held Calloc off till the end of the evening, when they walked home in the summer moonlight, Renée Kérouac and ' that accursed beast of an Englishman ' side by side the whole long way.

Two days after, Cecil went off in one of the Kérouacs' boats alone for the day, ostensibly to fish and sketch, as he often did, and always in a certain favourite boat, sculling or sailing according as the wind sat.

He was good at boating ; he could manage a sailing vessel to the admiration of the Kérouac lads, who were bred on the water. It was enough for him, with his tired brain and unstrung nerves, to sit in the stern, holding tiller and sail-rope, and glide over the blue water, watching the play of light and shade on the sea, the flight of sea-birds, the bold and varying outline of the rocky coast, the inland glimpses of village and heath, and that blue dimness in the east, which was the Norman St. Michael's Mount. At starting Raoul Kérouac had prophesied that he would not get to St. Michael's and back that day ; Hoël Calloc, who was standing by, corroborated the prophecy, smiling darkly. Cecil did not care ; he only wanted to sail and dream in the pleasant weather.

After two or three hours' tranquil progress, he reached a little rocky island some distance from a rock-bound coast. Here he landed, making the boat fast to a spike of rock. The wind had fallen, and sculling in the June sunshine was hot work ; it was pleasanter to lie under the shadow of a rock and look up into the blue sky, and be lulled by waves plashing on the jagged base of the islet. He had with him a worn pocket Horace, but it failed to interest ; it belonged to the days before his breakdown, since which he had turned to fresher, less sophisticated writers. The soft croon of these dancing, foaming waves made a drowsy burden to vague, desultory thoughts, half day-dream, half reflection. When would he recover his mental health ? When recur to the old interests ? Was he the same man as the occupant of those chambers in which he had thought, laboured, loved, and suffered so much ? Everything connected with the law now seemed hateful from sheer mental weariness. What if he gave up

his profession ?   Literature was more
alluring ; he would set seriously to work on
a serious poem, a challenge to posterity.
How much had *she* to answer for all this ?
She was called Phyllis in ' Daffodil Songs,'
and accused of falsehood, treachery, cruelty,
and other crimes peculiar to her sex,
according to rejected lovers.

> ' Oh that I had never known
>   Lips of lustre so beguiling ;
> Eyes whose beauty turns to stone,
> Oh that I had never known !
> All my peace of mind is flown
>   Since I saw their cruel smiling ;
> Oh that I had never known
>   Lips of lustre so beguiling !'—

was one of the lyrics due to this faithless damsel ; it set itself to the rhythmic
burden of crooning waves, and he was
comforted.   Phyllis, who went by another
name in society, was known to have
admired these poetic records of her mis-
deeds.   She had deliberately angled for her
poet, blown hot and cold, brought him on
and kept him off, never allowed him to
come to a formal proposal, and finally

thrown him over for the laggard lover whose halting advances she had intended to spur by jealousy. Everybody knew that Marlowe had been used as a decoy to bring the rich and titled suitor to the point; and all this, of course, was very sad and bad.

This catastrophe had been the last straw beneath which his health had given way, though the strenuous pursuit of pleasure, learning, and literature combined, on a vegetable diet, had been the more potent cause. Suppose that Phyllis had smiled kindly instead of cruelly. ' Good Lord !' he reflected, ' I might have been a married man this day, or at least booked for marriage.' The idea of this escape was soothing. After all, it is often a lucky thing to have one's heart broken. He had taken the love-fever, recovered, and would have it no more. That was well. The bitterness of the Phyllis refusal had arisen from wounded pride ; he had never felt for her a tithe of what he felt for his mother. To be sure, that was not to be expected; but in sober truth he had never loved her at all. She had attracted him with all the skill of a finished coquette; her beauty had charmed him, she had fired his imagination and kindled his pride, but not his heart. No woman could ever do that, he was quite sure.

Marriage would be a serious inconvenience to the youngest of several sons of a comparatively poor man. Love in a cot has few charms for a man of fastidious tastes and many needs, with his way to make in the world; besides, the favourite son of Susan Marlowe had formed a standard of womanly perfection which could never be reached. Like a true-born Englishman, he never expressed, and was only dimly conscious of, his strong attachment for his mother. Once, he remembered, when he was a little boy there had been a sad time, when the house was very still, and strange people crept noiselessly from room to room and he was banished from his mother's presence. For the first time in his life he had seen grown people crying—which always frightens children —and wondered what they were doing to her in her distant, hushed room. Grave, unknown men were at her bedside day and night; once there was blood on their hands; they were no doubt hurting her and keeping her shut up. He decided to kill them, with which intent he stole a knife from the nursery table—it was very blunt—and hid it successfully in his bed. In the night he got up, a little four-year-old boy in a little white shirt, and stole, in mortal terror of ghosts, witches, demons, ogres, goblins, and other delights, through the dark house to her door, which stood ajar.

Within, a woman was nodding by a shaded lamp; on the bed lay a shrouded, dark-haired figure very still. He crept in under the bed with the knife ready in a small trembling fist. His father stole softly in and looked upon the still form. The little son heard him cry and saw the nurse lead him quickly away. Then, dropping his weapon, the boy climbed on the bed and clasped and kissed the motionless, scarcely breathing figure again and again.

' Mother,' he cried, ' mother, mother !'

Then the mother woke and lived, revived, not killed, by the shock from which they had so carefully guarded her, actually recalled to life by the child's cry. Afterwards she told how the piteous, helpless cry pierced through an infinite black, blank nothingness in which she had lost herself, and evoked a rush of returning life with the feeling of the child's need. Yet quiet, the doctors said, was her only chance.

The idol of Cecil's infancy became, as he grew up, his best and most congenial friend, whose deep, silent, unswerving devotion, the strongest feeling of a strong nature, made the core of his life. He read her last letter again under the summer sky; it was worth re-reading. It contained no terms of endearment, but many shrewd thoughts and sparkling comments, and the frank confidence of friend to friend. Then he drowsed and dozed in the sunny salt air, and finally fell fast asleep.

The sun had traversed a large arc in the sky when he woke and went to unmoor his boat, which was nowhere to be found. The painter was still fast to the rock, but the boat attached to it had sunk. With much labour she was hauled up and found to have four holes in her bottom. Oars, mast and sail were gone; there was nothing to calk the boat with; the rocky shore was deserted; no vessel was near. The only thing to be done was to sit like Robinson Crusoe, but dinnerless and coatless, and watch for some sign of humanity on sea or shore.

Vessels appeared in the offing one after

the other, but none came near enough to perceive his feeble signalling.

The day wore away, the sun set most gloriously in the western waters, the darkness fell. The sea-birds' wailing was long since stilled; the lights in a village some way inland went out one by one; the clear sky was thronged with stars. What a situation for a poet!—alone on a rock amid the waste of surging waters, with dim surf-fringed shores faintly seen in pale starlight, nowhere any sign of humanity, only Nature in unclothed majesty, vast, lonely, calm. The song of summer waves, murmuring on in soft, continuous undertones, and blending with the spheral harmony all night long, might fire the feeblest imagination and make the most prosaic people hear the singing of distant mermaidens and watch the light dance of shadowy elves with the trembling waves.

But it was cold beneath the clear starry sky, the light airs skimming the wave-crests were sharp, the poet was hungry, and his bones ached; at full tide the spray drenched him. He would rather have been comfortably tucked up under a pile of eider-downs in a wooden bed-place. Those wet angular rocks made a poor couch for one cramped by long inaction, though it had been possible to sleep on them at low tide in the sunshine.

The stars wheeled very, very slowly by in their long and stately procession above the dark waters, which grew colder and colder ; but their rear-guard came, and they paled at last. Then the Norman coast showed purple black against a gray pallor, which grew to a pure beryl and changed to crimson and orange, violet and gold ; little waves leapt up in the changing light ; the dark sea rim and darker coast gradually brightened as the sun rose full-orbed above them. Cecil, drenched and in his shirt-sleeves, heard his teeth chatter, and felt his marrow turned to ice. He kept on the eastern face of his sea-castle to catch the sun-rays, and thought of buckwheat *crêpes* and hot coffee, and the pile of warm feather-beds in the turret-chamber.

The sunshine was strong and hot by the time a little fishing-smack saw him, fetched him off his rock and took him back to St. Brileuc, calking and towing the wrecked boat. By that time he was beyond eating the rye bread and cheese they had on board, and their hard cider scarcely refreshed him.

Gabriel Kérouac went down to the beach to look at the boat, and examined her carefully. 'Calloc's work,' he said on returning to the house.

Marlowe dragged his stiffened limbs to the feather-beds, which he found almost as angular as the granite rocks, and quite as cold. He could not eat, so Mère Suzanne gave him a hot tisane and recommended him to Ste. Anne d'Auray.

After some hours of troubled dozing, he sprang off the piled feather-beds, wide awake and restless. His bones ached, he felt as if made of mingled fire and air, and went out in the afternoon sunshine to walk off his stiffness and calm his mental excitement and confusion.

'Well, I must take myself off,' he thought, 'and then perhaps that beast Calloc will leave the poor girl in peace. Jealous of me! Gabriel not surprised! The villagers talking! Good Lord! I hope it mayn't come to Renée's ears. I should like a couple of rounds with Master Höel Calloc; I've wasted time enough here.'

The mental exaltation went off with the walk, and presently he leant against a mænhir and looked out upon the sea sparkling in the broad June light. Infinite loneliness and unspeakable sadness fell upon him there. The woman latent in every man awoke, as she often does at the approach of death or deadly sickness, and filled him with a vague, pitying tenderness. The sorrows of oppressed mankind through countless ages gathered and rolled sky-high over him, like a huge

Atlantic wave. When would cruelty and tyranny cease? How much longer would the weak be trampled beneath the feet of the strong?

He was passing slowly and painfully inland, when a sudden shriek of terror, followed by a crash of broken pottery, a dull thud and the crackling of bushes, arose from beneath the birch-trees by the stream, whence he once heard the Corregan's song, and whither he now plunged in hot haste.

CHAPTER V.

DASHING down into the glen, he came upon a sight which made his blood tingle to the finger-tips. Renée Kérouac, all dishevelled and bleeding, was struggling with all her might—which was considerable—in the grasp of Hoël Calloc, who, with infuriated face and blazing eyes, was clutching the thick masses of her long hair in one hand and savagely striking her with the *pen-bas*, or cudgel, he held in the other.

He was certainly not the first lover whose confidence in the softening qualities of stick (commonly reserved for post-nuptial endearments) led him to make use of it in courting a wife. He may never have heard of Duke William of Normandy's effectual employment of similar high-handed proceedings in winning the heart of Matilda (who doubtless reflected on the convenience of having a hard-hitter for a life-long protector in those hard-hitting days); or he may himself have originated this forcible style of courtship, finding gentler methods futile, and being himself chiefly answerable to such striking arguments.

But he had found rather a tougher subject than he anticipated in the stout-hearted, strong-armed girl, who, besides Hoël Calloc's fierce wooing, and ghosts, fairies, evil omens, and such-like, feared nothing. Cecil had seen her grasp the tiller and direct the trimming of the sail on the day when that sudden squall came up, and the tide was running in strong with the wind. The boat was all but on the rocks on that occasion, and the Kérouac brothers, giving up all for lost, were tearing their long hair, weeping, and fiercely expostulating with all their saints.

'Our Renée is a brave girl,' Gabriel observed to Marlowe when all were safe ashore ; 'she never loses her head. But for her, we should have been on the rocks, and then—good-night ! Strong, too : see how straight she kept the boat's head. The kind of wife any man would find useful.'

It was Renée who had so adroitly thrown the sheet over the mad bull's horns and blinded him, when men were flying right and left through the village. 'A sensible girl !' her father then said, returning to the scene and wiping the sweat of flight from his forehead.

'I'll teach you to have fine English lovers !' Calloc was shouting, to the accompaniment of his savage blows ; ' I'll teach you to '—this, that, and the other—' you ' —this, that, etc.—to the full extent of his most nauseous vocabulary, when the *pen-bas* suddenly flew from his hand and his arm cracked under a blow from an unseen fist. A second blow, straight from the shoulder, caught him on the side of his head and tumbled him over into the bracken, where he lay perfectly still out of sheer amazement.

'Now get up and let me thrash you,' cried Marlowe, towering pale and fierce-eyed above the prostrate form.

'Blessed St. Anne of Auray!' ejaculated Hoël, with chattering teeth and eyes that seemed all whites ; 'can a ghost hit so hard ?'

'Get up, you brute !' shouted Cecil in good plain English, while Calloc stammered out Breton invocations, prayers, and curses, as he lay shivering. 'Get up, before I take you by the scruff of your accursed neck and pound you to a jelly !'

He stooped for this purpose, when Hoël, divining it, leaped with one loud, long, complicated, and most unearthly yell to his feet and fled, as if pursued by ten thousand demons, his hat off, his long coarse black hair streaming in the wind, followed and favoured with a couple of parting kicks by Cecil, who then, reserving the pleasure of thrashing him for the future, turned back to the distressed damsel so timely delivered.

The miserable Calloc probably never made better use of his legs than on this occasion, nor probably was a more abject embodiment of terror ever beheld by mortal man than this fugitive lover. St. Pol, St. Michel, and, in short, every saint in Brittany were called upon, and promised everything a saint could need or wish for services to be rendered. Like all his countrymen, Calloc was accustomed to ghosts and spectres in every variety. Every year of his life he had seen doors left open and tables spread by hearths for the comfort of the poor souls wandering homeless in the November mist and chill on the *jour des morts*, but never till this sunshiny day had he the least suspicion of the vigour with which a ghost could

kick and hit straight and clean from the
shoulder.

Only the day before he had sent this
accursed Englishman to the bottom of the
sea, and here the fellow was, just as things
were being comfortably arranged between
himself and his sweetheart, visible and
audible — which might be expected of
ghosts at proper times and in proper
places—but, alas! how tangible—which
ghosts are never expected to be—inter-
rupting honest courtship and spoiling sport
in this unpleasant manner! Catholic ghosts
are poor enough companions for an honest,
lusty fellow, fond of gavottes, cider, songs,
and revel, but heretics newly killed and
unburied are the very devil.

' Blessed Ste. Anne d'Auray, you don't
catch me drowning another heretic for all
the sweethearts in Brittany!' he vowed, as
he fled and fled, starting at every sound,
stumbling over sticks and stones, briars
and brambles, springing to his feet again
and running on and on. Whither the

unlucky Calloc fled is not known—he may, indeed, still be fleeing at this moment for all that is recorded to the contrary—but he certainly fled out of the lives of both the distressed damsel and her deliverer, and out of the ken of his native commune, in which a belief subsequently arose that he rushed blindly into the Baie des Trépassés, where his spirit roams in perpetual unrest, howling and shrieking in those sudden storms that overtake and wreck ill-starred vessels there. But of Calloc's fate Cecil thought little, when he turned back to the Andromeda he had delivered more by the Medusa shield he unconsciously carried than by actual fight.

Renée was sitting, breathless and trembling, on a mossy stone amid the shards of her broken butter-jar, her splendid curtain of hair hanging tangled and blood-stained about her, stanching the blood with her apron. She looked like a Banshee in evil case.

'What was it all about, Renée?' he

asked, after examining the wound, which
he washed with water from the stream
and bound with his handkerchief and a
strip of his shirt-sleeve. 'Wait till I
catch that beast Calloc,' he added, with
grim satisfaction; 'I don't think he will
touch you again, you poor child!'

'It was about you,' she replied, looking
up with that in the wistful brilliance of
her large eyes which made his heart throb
strangely, and sent a thrill of mingled pain
and pleasure through him. 'Dear sir, do
not give him a chance; he means the
worst. He is a bad, violent man; he will
stick at nothing.'

'What am I to Hoël Calloc?' he asked,
in a voice that sounded strange to himself.
'Dear Renée—dear child!' he laid his
hand, trembling with a sudden return
of fever, upon her shoulder, 'it is you
whom he persecutes—you, who are de-
fenceless.'

Renée's eyes fell; she drew the veil of
hair before her face, shrinking and shudder-

ing beneath the burning touch on her shoulder.

' Monsieur !' she sighed, 'oh, monsieur !' then a great sob shook her and the tears rained hotly down.

' Poor Renée—poor little bird !' he said, in a tremulous yet full voice, ' do not be afraid, I am strong enough to defend us both. I will take care of you, dear Renée.'

' Oh, I am not afraid—only for *you*. He is so jealous,' she replied in quick, fluttering gasps. ' He has no right. I never listened to him—never ! I never cared until——' A fresh burst of tears.

' But why do you cry, why does my pretty bird cry ? I am here,' he said, sliding to the rock by her side beneath the birches. Renée was silent, trembling, both in heaven and in hell—pleasure so wild and pain so subtle had never touched her till now—Cecil half dazed, conscious of a temptation he had neither will nor power to flee. The birken shadows moved, and, gliding off a strip of rippling stream, left its brown depths bare to the sunshine, weaving golden meshes there.

Spellbound these two sat, so still that birds hopped at their feet and poised on branches near, and the wagtail paced serenely to and fro before them, wrapped in profound meditation on affairs wagtailian. Renée at last rose silently and began to gather the massive folds of her hair together; Cecil rose then, but slowly and heavily, and tried to help her bind the tresses, when the pride of the Breton girl awoke and she dragged them fiercely from his profaning touch, asking him in plain terms what he meant by his impudence in daring to touch a girl's hair.

Then the bushes rustled, a man's step was heard, and Michel Kérouac appeared.

'What is this, monsieur the painter?' he cried.

'A man was beating your daughter. I knocked him down; that was all.'

'The man was Hoël Calloc, monsieur.
Why was he beating my girl? We are
not blind ; we can see at noon of a sunny
day. Hoël Calloc has wherewithal to
marry my daughter. He is frugal and
industrious, monsieur the painter.'

'He is a *brute* !' shouted Cecil. 'He
dragged her by the hair and struck her
brutally. Look at the poor child's face
and dress ; she is covered with blood.'

'She deserved it,' returned Kérouac
grimly. 'Hoël is a good fellow. He is
a good match. For you, monsieur, it
must be ended.'

By this time Renée, blushing hotly
with mingled shame and defiance, had
bound up her hair under her cap, picked
up her burdens and walked on, knitting
as she went.

Then Michel Kérouac followed her
homewards, keeping her well in sight and
accompanied by Cecil, whose pulses beat
in fierce tumults of indignation and
passion, while his dark face glowed, his

strong brows knit, and he kept a sombre
silence all the way.

'It was Calloc,' Michel said as they
went along ; 'Calloc who sunk the boat,
meaning to drown you. It must be
ended '—a proposition to which no one
was more ready to agree than Cecil,
though he did not say so. 'It must be
ended,' Kérouac repeated angrily. Cecil
assented with a nod. 'It must be ended,
Monsieur Cecil,' Père Michel repe ted
again, after a long stretch of ground had
been gone over in grim silence.

He groaned within himself, thinking of
the improbability of Cecil's marrying his
daughter and the inconvenience of sending
him away and so losing the price of his
board and lodging, therefore he stimulated
his lagging virtue by this reiterated 'It
must be ended.'

Cecil, indifferent to the good man's
struggle between greed and duty, his
daughter and his ducats, was aware of
nothing but Renée walking ahead in

sunlight and leaf-shadow with her usual
free step and proud carriage. His brain
was on fire, his eyes glowed with a
smouldering flame, his pulses throbbed.
Renée's well-set-up, strong and supple
figure assumed heroic proportions in his
imagination ; she became an embodiment
of the peasantry he loved, as Clärchen was
to Egmont a symbol of the people for
whom he died.

For the moment it seemed strange that
all that is picturesque and poetic, pathetic
and noble in the tillers of the soil—their
princely simplicity and racy speech, which
tastes of sighing winds, of fields and dew,
their wholesome plain-spoken purity, their
sun-burnt vigour, their many denials and
great toils, their honest and loyal affections, should take mortal shape and walk
before him in the form of one pretty
country girl who loved him—strange yet
inevitable. From his cradle he had
studied and loved English rustics, reputed
stolid, but always with a breath of poetry

for those who understand them ; if he loved those homely folk, how much more should he love these, who breathed an air teeming with romance in a country whose every dell and forest was haunted by fairies and sacred with legend and song.

Centuries of injustice, endurance and toil looked out of the depths of this young, brave, over-burdened woman's blue, darkly-fringed eyes, the glow of many hundred Junes was in her full red lips, and he knew that she loved him.

'Do you mean to marry my daughter?' asked Père Michel when they arrived at the ruined castle and Renée disappeared within the dark doorway.

He woke from his reverie with a start. '*Marry* her !' he cried, facing about, and looking the father in the face. Michel Kérouac made no reply, but his look was impressive, and Cecil's not less so. 'God knows,' the latter replied after awhile, 'I meant no wrong. I must go,' he added, after another pause and exchange of regards on either part ; ' I will go at once,' he repeated, staggering, pale and large-eyed, into the ruined hall, where Mère Suzanne was singing to the hum of her wheel,

> ' " Mother, haste thee ! O mother, spread,
>   If thou lovest me, my death-bed ;

> ' " Me the fairy has looked to death ;
>   In three days I yield my breath—" '

when the sound of his fall interrupted wheel and song, and she rose and caught him.

' Blessed St. Pol, it is the fever !' she cried. ' What wonder—all night on the rocks in the wet, fasting !'

Then he was carried by strong arms to the turret-chamber, where for a few days he lay fighting at hand-grips with death.

Mother and daughter tended him carefully night and day, administering *tisanes* and sudorifics with untiring devotion, while he raved in delirium, sank in stupor, or battled painfully for breath. It was a hard task for these hardy women, who accepted it as they accepted the innumerable ills of their hard life. The tired, hard-worked mother sometimes drowsed and dozed in the long nights, when the delirious patient would leap from his bed and harm himself; but the equally tired and hard - worked daughter, worn with fear and upborne by the passion of devotion, never so much as nodded or suffered her aching eyelids to droop, and when he would have sprung from his painful bed, humoured his wild fancies, and held him down with strong but gentle force. It was Renée's hand that led him safely over the dark and difficult passage from death to life.

One night he woke partially from a death-like stupor to see dimly, as in a dream, the charming figure of his young nurse kneeling by his bed. Her hands were clasped in supplication, her uplifted face showed pale in the dim lamp-light; she was praying for his life.

The grand simplicity of prayer straight from the heart makes it intelligible with-

out words. In spite of the foreign tongue,
Marlowe divined it all: the vow of pilgrimage, the sacrifice of her sole earthly
possession, her magnificent hair, the offer
of her life for his. Under the stress of
this pure and fiery passion and ardent
faith, Cecil's nature quivered and shook,
something stirred and woke deep within
him, a vital thrill struck along the death-
chilled currents of his blood—they turned
from their icy stagnation and flowed back
towards health—and, closing his eyes in
blissful assurance of new life, he fell into
a deep and healing sleep.

As he grew better, his heart beat
happily at the sound of Renée's approach,
and his face fell when Mère Suzanne took
her place—Renée's touch was so gentle,
her voice so clear, her intuition of his
wants so perfect. To lie still in his weakness and look upon her, as she moved in
his service and sat by the deep turret-
window knitting or spinning with untiring
industry, was happiness. She would sing

at his desire, and her voice was sweet ;
she would tell him endless legends, and
with every day her beauty and the charm
of her fresh and ardent nature grew upon
him.   Later on, some questions of his
brought out the fact that her daily hard
work had gone on as usual while she was
nursing him, and she had not even missed
for many mornings going to Mass.   What
endurance, what devotion was here !

A few weeks later, Cecil Marlowe, fully
restored to vigour, awoke one golden
summer evening, as if from a long, dim,
half-waking dream, to the full and conscious enjoyment of mental strength.

Tables were spread beneath trees that
formed part of the once beautiful forest
in which the Sieurs de Brigny had been
used to hunt ; peasants in the different
costumes of their communes, costumes
picturesque and full of colour, sat in
groups in the shade, clustered about the
well-laden tables, or danced to the music
of the *biniou*.   Sabots had given place to

buckled shoon, jackets and bodices were gaily trimmed, and the latter often made of rich stuff ; great oaken coffers by bed-places had been ransacked for the richest clothing ; men's *bragous bras* of velvet, and women's skirts with many rows of trimming, brocades, ribbons and silver ornaments, had been brought out from darkness into the sunlight.

Renée, clad in silver tissue and cloth of gold, her bodice and head-gear glittering in the sun-rays, sat beneath an oak, quiet and subdued amid the mirth, as became a bride ; Marlowe, an incongruous figure in evening dress, his snowy linen lavendered by the young bride's own hands, stood near her with folded arms, and that sudden look of awakening. Sea-gulls sailed homewards, now with flapping wings and visible effort, now gliding on stirless pinion, straight and calm as floating cloudlets, their short white bodies gleaming bright against the blue sky and bluer sea, freest and happiest of living

things.   Here was the airy circling of
slender swallows, with purple flash of
glossy wings ; larks' songs, in fullest
compass and most lavish variety of quick
melody, rose joyously above the low, soft,
infinitely peaceful murmur of the sea, the
continuous boom of which, hushed though
it was, penetrated and mellowed even the
rustic dance-music and the shouts and
laughter of the dancers.

The sea was of a wine-like transparency;
away in the west it was molten gold ; the
rose and purple of sunset already tinged
the tumbling snow of surf-lines and crim-
soned the jutting eastern cliffs.   Tranquil
as the waves were in their evening repose,
they broke upon those outer rocks in
showers of soft high-flying foam, with a
gentleness inexpressibly soothing ; they
caught rose and lilac bloom, and tossed
them over the rocks in spray-fountains ;
yonder a vision of unutterable glory glided
towards the glorious west, a full-rigged
three-masted ship, its set sails of Tyrian

dye, its hull burnished gold. The scent of hay, clover and trodden turf mingled with the keen salt sea-breath; the village, with its massive quaint church, became a jewel in the glory ; woods and trees wore their thickest foliage steeped in light. The year had developed its fullest splendour, the day was at its loveliest moment, Marlowe had a sudden sense of the richest possibilities of life and of his own nature, his heart leapt with the passion of poetry and with that conviction so dear to youth that the world was before him to conquer.

He turned and looked at Renée, whose face was radiant in sunset glow. She had been the chief figure in that long dim, waking dream, and yet, alas ! she was no dream, but a breathing flesh-and-blood reality, and—his wife.

CHAPTER VI.

THE WEDDING FEAST.

MARRYING, like hanging, dying and being born, is so easily and quickly done, and usually in such lightness of heart and from motives so sudden and slight, that its irrevocable nature and life-long consequences are not often realized till too late.

Gratitude, the poetic charm so easily cast on a vivid imagination, admiration, compunction, and pity for the simple and guileless woman who loved him with such unselfish devotion, together with a remote underlying conviction that marriage was never intended to form a serious part of his life—the old cant, a

man's episode, a woman's life—had been
the chief causes, on the part of the bridegroom, of that picturesque wedding.
Nothing seemed of consequence to one who
had for the time laid moral responsibility
aside, to a mind so much overstrained
and languid with the reaction which is
nature's instinctive medicine for over-
tension. But marriage, after all, is
marriage ; it is one thing to promise
marriage and quite another to go to
church and hear solemn words accompanying solemn rites, and come out from
the cool dimness and incense-laden atmosphere into the broad every-day sunshine,
bound, not for a brief holiday, but for life.

These reflections, which had startled the
bridegroom for a moment in church, were
danced and laughed aside for a while ; the
full waking did not come till later.

Michel Kérouac was far too good a
father not to drain as many cups of his
oldest cider as he could at his only
daughter's wedding, in consequence of

which this worthy man, in an access of bibulous emotion, took Marlowe by the shoulder with a loud ' Hé, gendre !' and tried to kiss him. Yet Cecil actually was the son-in-law of this French peasant, drunk or sober ; he could not expect the manners of English gentlemen from him.

What would his father and mother think of the present scene ? The latter was now staying with her mother at her birthplace in Cornwall ; she had received a jesting account of her son's adventure in the boat, the illness subsequent to which had been translated into a troublesome cold. For all Cecil knew, she might at this moment be looking on that very sea incarnadined by the setting sun, from the opposite shore, which was so like this. Mother and son might actually be facing each other, their glances separated only by those miles of blue sea air ; she might be looking south, thinking of him, as he looked north, thinking of her. So he thought, with dark looks and troubled brow, an incongruous black blot on that many-coloured, sunburnt pastoral, the centre of a family feast in which neither his mother nor any of his kin had any part.

'Can you still be in that enchanted Brittany?' the mother's last letter ran— 'I address to Rennes as usual in the full expectation of receiving fresh directions in your next. We are terrified at the thought of going to so seductive a place as your Brittany; at our age the General and I might take root and grow into the soil. It is not the Corregan that we dread : she would not waste her enchantments upon gray hairs or her own sex ; but what if we should step into the enchanted circle in which Merlin sleeps spell-bound? I hope you have not fallen into this unawares, because the victims of that enchantment become invisible. Then we have serious thoughts of the Pyrenees for the autumn, and hope you will join us. I want to hear that wondrous horn in the pass of Roncesvalles. That magic music

harms no one, unlike your Corregan with
her :

> ' " Me on the instant thou shalt wed,
>   Or in three days shalt be dead " '

—a bold-faced jig, making love to other
people's sweethearts and husbands.   Then
I must see the Alhambra, and the
General wants to prowl on Peninsular
battle-fields.   Some day you will come
home and find an entrenched camp and
fortified kitchen-garden at Cottesloe, and
your father, à la Uncle Toby, bombarding
my pet conservatories with cabbages.'

How dear Cottesloe seemed to Marlowe
at that moment, and how delightful was
the vision conjured up of the bluff, kind-
hearted General on his hobby.   The
kitchen-garden had actually been fortified
one Christmas holidays after a heavy
snowfall, and Cecil, though willing enough
to take part in either storm or defence of
that stronghold, had incurred disgrace
from his lack of interest in the principles

on which the siege works were constructed.

'You'll never be a soldier, boy!' his father had grumbled.

'I hope not,' he answered, to the General's amazement.

'This comes of letting him be too much with his mother,' the latter thought.

'Ah, my dear,' Lady Susan was saying on that bright summer evening on the Cornish shore to Cynthia Brande, just now in quarantine in a village near with a detachment of little Forde-Cusackes, who were convalescing from one of the infantile maladies they were perpetually taking, 'sons are very trying. I often feel like a hen watching her ducklings on a pond. It is useless to cackle; the brood will and must swim. You cannot fight Nature. I am uneasy about Cecil and his solitary stagnation in Brittany. He writes so little. If he were a daughter I should be with him, of course, and see that he did everything he ought to re-establish his health.'

' And give him pills,' added Cynthia softly, with a plaintive sigh.

' You ungrateful girl !—you know that you owe your present bloom to those pills !'

' *And* the morning camomile, dear Lady Susan,' corrected Cynthia. ' Pray remember the camomile. But surely Mr Cecil has been much more with you than your soldier and sailor sons ?'

' True. When my husband was in the Crimea with my eldest boy, a mere child, and my poor little middie was in the Baltic, it was more than I could bear, and Hugh let Cecil leave school and stay with me under a tutor. The other boys were at school. Cynthia, I can never tell you what comfort I had in the child through all that awful time. Think what it must be to have a husband and two children, mere children, on active service for two years ! One never dared let one's

self think. Never marry a soldier, unless
your heart is of iron and your nerves of
brass, my dear. I brought Cecil home
from India as a baby, too, and had to
leave my husband behind. Oh, it was
hard! But all that made the child
dearer. We have been so much alone
together and have so many thoughts in
common. His father never understood
him. " Because we have no girl, don't
turn Cecil into one," he used to say, and
was sometimes rougher with the boy
on that account, fearing he would become
effeminate. The dear General has an
idea that what interests me must per-
force be womanish. What a triumph
for me when Cecil thrashed the tinker!
Hugh confessed then that I had not made
him unmanly.'

'And the General is very proud of him
now,' added Cynthia.

'Proud? Oh yes, now! But one
sadly misses a daughter. Do you know
that I speak to you of things on which

I can speak to no one, not even to
Cecil ?'

' I am glad,' she replied, ' very glad.'

Both women were silent then, looking
with earnest eyes over the flushed calm
sea, away from the blaze of the sunset,
towards Brittany, where the mirth of that
rustic wedding was growing boisterous as
night drew on.   Cynthia was thinking
that a real daughter would have seen less
of Lady Susan's inmost heart than had
been revealed to her, and she appreciated
this, while she wondered how that honest,
unimaginative soldier, Hugh Marlowe,
had captivated her friend's youth, and
felt that such a union must have had
tragic elements for a woman with so
keen a hunger for sympathy as Lady
Susan.

' You know, Cynthia,' sighed the latter,
after awhile, and Cynthia saw that her
eyes were wet, ' I am a little uncanny.
It is part of my Cornish blood.   I should
have been burnt as a witch a couple

of centuries ago. I have presentiments and the creeps and the jumps and all sorts of nonsense.'

' Nerves ?' Cynthia gently suggested.

' And — well, I am *sure* that something is happening to Cecil to-night.'

' Dear Lady Susan,' returned Cynthia, gently pressing her hand, ' it is not only the Cornish blood and the infection of your Cornish cousins' society, but the Cornish air and—dare I suggest it ?— clotted cream.'

Lady Susan smiled. ' I cannot forget him a moment,' she replied, ' and I hear the bell toll. You know that is my warning. He is in grave peril.'

Meanwhile Cecil went on gazing from the Breton shore with an immense yearning ; it was as if some unseen power were drawing his soul across the calm many - coloured sea - plains. He had lingered long enough in this drowsy, dreamy corner of the earth, among simple superstitious labourers. The mental re-

pose had done its work, the no more
needed quiet had lost its charm ; he felt
that he must be up and away into the
wide world, into the storm of action,
shaking off all the memories and associations of this healing place, as one shakes
off the shadows of dreams on waking to
broad sunlight.   A great sigh burst
from him ; he turned and looked at the
revelry, which was beginning to bore him.
That first wedding at which he had tried
to put things straight between Hoël and
Renée had been amusing to him as an
outsider ; but now that he was one of the
masquers, he saw the wrong side of the
show, the tinsel and tawdriness.   Among
the masquers ?   Alas ! marriage is a very
long masquerade, and who masques as
bridegroom can only change his *rôle* for
one in the pageant of death — which
could scarcely be grimmer, Cecil thought.
He looked at Renée, who was talking
with the village priest, a short, dark-
faced Breton, raised only by his call-

ing, and the knowledge necessary to it, above his flock. The many-coloured sunset had faded, leaving the bride in a chill, harsh light, in which her silver tissues and gold brocade looked tawdry and stagey. And this was Lady Susan's daughter-in-law ! And the General's ! 'You infernal young fool!' he could almost hear his father exclaim. It was worse than folly, it was crime ; and there was no place for repentance now. He was half minded to fly then and there in the sudden pain of coming to himself like the prodigal—among the swine—he bitterly thought, loathing the tipsy hilarity of the men. And this was the peasantry he had loved and seen typified in Renée ! It was too late to fly, and yet would it not be better ? Far better, had he but known—Renée's heart would have broken, nothing more.

Just then Renée turned with a look in her deep eyes that was like the infinite gaze of the myriad-starred night. The bridal costume might be tawdry, and even soiled and discoloured, but a warm, loyal, and pure heart beat beneath it—a life hung upon his with a trust he would never betray.

When the wedding festivities were at last ended, and that was not done in one day, or even in two, Marlowe took his young bride away for a day's sail, and landed with her in a quiet cove, where they might pass the noon-day heat in the shade of tall pink cliffs.   He had, until the marriage papers were drawn up, been known only as Monsieur Cecil, and supposed to be an obscure painter, such as sometimes found their way into those remote parts.   Now his full name, parentage and profession were known to the Kérouacs. To-day, while they rested under those pink rocks, he explained to Renée as fully as he could the rank and prejudices of his family, the fact that he dared not yet avow his marriage, and the necessity of preparing her for a very different position from that in which she had been reared. For that summer she might remain in Brittany to spare her parents the sudden wrench of losing her, but she must do no rough field-work and learn much. Then she must go to school, and learn more. He, in the meantime, must make a position for himself, which he could scarcely do without his father's support and the allowance he would probably withdraw from him in anger on hearing of this unequal marriage.

All this was carefully and with some difficulty explained to Renée in the French that he spoke haltingly and she understood but partially, and eked out with often mis-applied Breton phrases, and the final and full comprehension of the situation brought sorrow to her heart and troubled her large blue eyes. It meant the annihilation of her whole previous life, the destruction of old associations and ideals and the slow acquisition of new standards of thought

and conduct. It meant with most literal
fulness that she should ' forget her own
people and her father's house,' and set
forth alone on an unknown sea. She
accepted this inevitable pain without a
murmur, only hoping that she might
in time fashion herself in such form as
would please her husband, fearing sadly
that she would never reach the standards
required of her.

She was only too compliant and
anxious to serve and please him ; it
irritated him and hurt his self-respect
to see her proffering small services and
treating him as the Bretonnes treated
their husbands ; servility was bad enough
in others, but in her it was unbear-
able. Renée Kérouac might do much
with grace and propriety which in ' my
wife ' was intolerable.

The marriage-ring had scarcely been
on her finger an hour before the glamour
surrounding the pretty peasant maiden
had faded and she had appeared in the

gray hues of everyday prose, a devoted, well-behaved girl, widely sundered from all his interests and hopes, no longer even typifying that imaginative and simple-hearted peasantry from which the fascination had also departed, leaving plain facts and defects in glaring light. There is much potency in the marriage-ring.

The young couple had eaten their simple repast of cheese, buckwheat galettes, eggs and cider just before this first marital lecture was delivered. Renée then took her distaff, which had its special loop in her bodice to hold it when not in use, and was diligently spinning. She listened and span and span without ceasing, though some tears dropped on her spinning, as she looked sadly out to sea. The tears were like scalding drops on her husband's heart; he felt the world-wide cruelty of husbands to wives more burningly than ever now that he had entered that great army of oppressors. The one inexpiable cruelty was the marriage itself; the only thing now was to make the best of it.

'Renée, my Renée!' he cried, stroking the warm sun-tinted cheek, over which the tears flowed, 'it is cruel for you, child, but indeed it is best.'

'Yes,' she replied with a sad acquiescence that smote his heart; 'I know it. I will try hard to make me fit to show to your lady mother.'

The hour that followed was sweet to Renée, and the homeward voyage in the tranquil evening, when the breeze had died away and each took an oar, as sweet. Many such sailings took place, but each left the husband sadder. As long as the wife could remain mentally in Brittany, among homespun interests, local superstitions and legends, she was companionable and intelligent, but to all outside those narrow limits she was deaf and dumb and blind. Marlowe had hitherto been too much occupied in bringing out the knowledge and intelligence of his Breton friends to trench upon the regions of their ignorance, and now the vast blanks he found in Renée's mind startled him. Even her beauty lost its charm, her lack of intellect reduced her to the level of a well-looking and respectable girl—nothing more.

She looked best in motion; standing up in the boat, managing the sails, springing lightly to land, rowing, walking with her free and graceful carriage and erect head. Then she was in her element; her supple, well-developed figure showed to advantage; the rich bloom in her cheek and lip, and the splendour of her violet—at times almost purple—eyes, had their full value; her rather large and labour-coarsened hands were unobserved. There was even a certain grandeur about her, the grandeur of simplicity. But in repose she was not graceful, because seldom quite at ease, and when bewildered or uninterested, her face had the peasant's heaviness, her eyes lost their liquid light, her colour seemed a little hard, her movements in small things were too strong.

It was, after all, the wife who interrupted the honeymoon *tête-à-tête*; she left him to fulfil her vow of pilgrimage to the shrine of Ste. Anne d'Auray.

The day after her departure he found himself at Cherbourg, drawing deep breaths of a relief that he knew would be only temporary. To watch the bustle and stir of the sea-port, to look at the shipping, the shops, the hotels, the people, acted as a sort of mental tonic.

'How could I have been such an unutterable fool?' he wondered, as the past few months died away from his mind like a dream. 'Why, in the name of all that is idiotic, did I do it?' Yet thousands and thousands of fairly happy marriages are entered upon with less motive than was his. People drift into marriage as casually as they turn aside to gather wildflowers.

Suddenly, in the thronged street, he heard his own name, and turned to see the face of a man in yachting serge, scowling upon him from beneath a peaked blue cap with true British good-fellowship.

'How are you?' Cecil growled in answer to the sole word 'Marlowe!' moving aside at the same time to let two French gentlemen rush frantically into each other's arms with mutual kisses and lifted hats.

'Good heavens! what asses these Frenchmen make of themselves!' commented the yachtsman. 'Beastly hole, Cherbourg! Are you staying here? No? Nor am I. That is the *Firefly* in the harbour, with my wife on board. Can't you dine with us to-night?'

CHAPTER VII.

To go on board the graceful schooner yacht lying at anchor in the harbour that evening was to the expatriated Englishman like returning to a pleasant home after long absence. The sea, in which the *Firefly's* sloping lines were reflected, was calm, the blue and gold day hushing towards its close; soft, scarcely perceptible, airs wafted a salt coolness from the water. The dainty pleasure-ship, the perfection of cleanliness and order, and the white-jacketed crew in broad hats with gold-lettered bands, looked English to the core. The yacht's people were old friends, Mrs. Willoughby being a pretty woman of three-and-thirty. A girl cousin was cruising with them, also a tall dragoon, whom Cecil knew, a merry lad fresh from school, and a spinster with a sense of humour.

After all, civilization has its charms. Wooden spoons, no forks, soup served in hollows carved in the table, cider and milk, buckwheat *crêpes* and rye bread, onions and sausages, are no doubt refreshing to one tired of civilization and smarting from female scorn ; but even these delights pall with time, and when Marlowe found himself dining in the white and gold saloon, he liked the sight of the table, with its gleam of silver, sparkle of glass, gloss of damask, bloom and odour of crimson and white roses, peaches and apricots.

These things and the noiseless and careful waiting, the well-cooked courses and well-selected wines, and, above all, the intercourse with equals, had a home-like charm and the freshness which follows abstinence. He had been out of the world long enough for the most out-worn topics to be interesting. He had seen neither the pictures, the books, the plays nor the beauties of the season; knew nothing of the latest Parliamentary doings, who had been singing in what operas, or— 'Oh, Mr. Marlowe, can this be possible ? are you not taking us in ?'—the pass to which things had come in Europe, two great German nations flying at each other's throats, rivals in strife most unholy and fratricidal. Well, yes, he had to confess that he was aware that war had broken out, but did not know how it had sped. Austria getting the worst of it? Really interesting ; he must certainly read up to date. The dragoon's brother had seen Königsgratz from the top of a church tower. Mr. Marlowe was quite a curiosity ; he ought to be put under a glass case, ticketed, and presented to a museum.

'Brittany must be a very attractive

country,' Mrs. Willoughby averred. 'We
have been debating where we should take
our next run ashore. What is there to
do in Brittany, Mr. Marlowe ?'

'Nothing—nothing whatever,' he replied hastily.

'Yet you have been a long time doing
it ?'

'Yes; you know I knocked up, over-
read and had the usual prescription—
neither do, think nor see anything whatever, or at least of the faintest interest,
for six months. So I went to Brittany
and did it.' He spoke quietly, but his
heart beat violently at the possibility of
people from his own world penetrating to
the solitudes which held his secret, and
he could not keep back a hot flush from
his sunburnt face, which was clean-shaven,
thus revealing the full play of his
features.

'Let us go to Brittany and do it too,'
said the pretty cousin. 'We are all
worn out and want rest.'

' *How* did you do nothing, Mr. Marlowe ?' continued the hostess. ' I have often thought I should like to do it ; pray tell us how the thing is done.'

' Very easy,' the ex-Harrovian replied : ' you lie on your back and smoke.'

' *We* can't lie on our backs and smoke, Harold,' objected the pretty cousin ; ' besides, we are not *all* reading for the Indian Civil Service.'

' I took an easel and pretended to paint,' Marlowe explained ; ' that is an effective way of doing nothing, as the experience of centuries proves. Oh no ! there is nothing to paint there, I assure you. As for " Druidic remains," you go to Carnac to see them, in the south. And for scenery the west coast, or the south. But the west is grandest ; the full force of the Atlantic has torn out the granite rocks and tossed them about like tennis-balls there.'

' Lady Susan was speaking of the Atlantic rollers on the Cornish coast. I suppose you know that charming girl she has been taking about — a Miss Brande ?'

He was glad to change the subject and to reflect that Renée would probably not use his name. He being M. Cecil, she would be Madame Cecil in common parlance. That whim of forgetting his name for the time was a lucky inspiration; nor was there any deceit in this incognito : the Kérouacs now knew his name and condition, which were inscribed in the marriage papers.

Coffee and cigars were served on deck in the balmy evening air ; just as they emerged from the saloon, the Angelus was borne in sweet and melancholy cadence across the harbour from many a belfry ashore, and the glories of day were dying from the western waters.

' Are not the Bretons very pious ?' Mrs. Willoughby asked, the ladies having come on deck. ' I have a vague notion that Brittany is a sort of daylight opera

in which pretty girls in costume are
always dancing with shadows and marrying chivalrous peasants.'

' A false impression. They are pious
indeed, but very, very tipsy, and, far
from being chivalrous, they despise and
ill-treat women, and make them thresh
corn and do field-work. And they are
very ignorant and superstitious, and dirtier
than it is possible for some people to
imagine.'

' Who would go to Brittany after this?'
the pretty cousin exclaimed.

' Cleanliness and costume never go
together,' commented the spinster.

' Piety and the picturesque are
associated with piggishness,' added Mrs.
Willoughby. ' Do you remember those
Neapolitans, Maud ?'

> ' O dolce Napoli,
> O suol' beato !'

somebody began to sing in an undertone,
and the rest took it up and sang it
through in harmony, gay and wholesome

singing in contrast with eldritch Breton melodies. When the stars looked out of the silvery blue sky the air turned a little chill and they returned to the saloon, which was bright with pendent silver lamps.

How wholesome was the music there, and how truly English! Mrs. Willoughby's ' Bid me discourse ' and ' Love has eyes ' to violin and piano ; the dragoon's 'Come into the garden, Maud,' in a passable tenor. Then the candidate for the Civil Service blundered cheerfully through ' The Stirrup-cup,' with an unblushing, ' Just give me C'; or, ' I say, do wait for a fellow, Miss Ormonde'; and the whole company joined in ' Here in cool grot.' There were no fatal Corregans singing people to death. And none of the party seemed concerned with Arthurian romance, or any of the devilries and witcheries connected with that saint and wizard haunted country. The sound of English voices and the soft slur of the

English *r* completed the wholesome charm of the evening.

'Over-work indeed!' commented the hostess to her spinster friend. 'Georgie Vivian, he meant. She used him shamefully.'

'Well, it is evident that he didn't take Georgie Vivian fatally, or even severely,' her friend returned; 'he has certainly recovered from her. Do you think I don't know the symptoms of the complaint?'

Early next morning Marlowe and his bag were rowed by the neat English yachtsmen out to the *Firefly*, and remained on board all day while they tacked about with a light breeze. Late in the evening he was rowed ashore to a little town on the south-west coast of Brittany, declining to go farther on account of an engagement to meet 'a friend.'

'I have done for myself,' he thought, waving a last farewell to the yacht as she stood off. 'My mother would be heart-broken if she knew.' Then he turned his face towards St. Brileuc to meet his young bride, and a few days later drew near to the familiar ruined tower. He knew that Renée must have returned, but his heart, instead of leaping up at the prospect of meeting her, sank like a stone. Presently he caught sight of a figure in the well-known costume — white apron and cap, dark short skirt, and dark stockings and sabots—and sighed ; but it proved to be not Renée, and he was relieved.

But what horror was this—a female in *bourgeoise* dress descending the steps to meet him ? Yes ; a female in a long green gown, expanded by a crinoline, which swayed its horrid hoops in its own ungainly fashion with every step uncertainly taken on high-heeled French boots; a female wearing a sort of yellowish cloak, and a pink bonnet of the spoon shape then in vogue, and carrying a parasol of some

terrible colour. The horror rose to a
nightmare when from beneath the dreadful
bonnet beamed the love-lit eyes of Renée,
her beauty disguised and insulted by this
hideous travesty of civilized garb.

'For heaven's sake, Renée!' he gasped,
unable to conceal his dismay, 'what have
you done to yourself?'

She drew herself up, smiling, unconscious of the horror she evoked, and
delighted to have surpassed his expecta-
tions in so readily becoming what he
wished her to be—an English lady.

He felt the pathos through the gro-
tesque, kissed her resignedly, and tried to
commend her; but the effort was beyond
him, and the poor young bride was cut to
the heart.

'I like you best as I first saw you,' he
explained gently, bidding her remove the
bonnet that he might see her in her old
familiar aspect. 'Good Lord!' he cried,
when she obeyed, 'where is your hair—
your beautiful hair?'

'Blessed St. Yves!' she replied, bursting into tears. 'It was for thee! I vowed it for thy life!'

All the black, bronze-tinted splendour had been ruthlessly cropped, leaving a short, thick, rebellious growth, which would neither curl nor lie down, but stood out spikily in every direction, giving her a wild and disordered air, that emphasized the ugliness of her attire.

'It was all I had!' she sobbed. 'I would have given my life, myself, the good God knows—yes, I would even have given my poor soul for thee!'

He understood her by the passion in her voice, though she spoke in dialect; he hated himself, he hated his life, he almost hated his innocent bride.

This burst of wounded love and disappointed hope was a prophecy of the perpetual pain he must bring her; his own wretchedness was a foretaste of the ever-recurring disgust in store for him. It would have been kinder to have left her

at the first, would even now perhaps be
kinder to leave her. In the meantime
here she was, sobbing vehemently, with a
good spice of rage mingled with her disappointment and heart-break, at their first
reunion. 'He will soon begin to beat
me now ; all the courting is over,' the
poor child thought, grieved to the heart
that the inevitable beating should begin
so early.

'Forgive me,' he said, laying his hand
gently on the bowed head, shorn of its
comeliness for his sake ; 'I had forgotten.
The hair was so beautiful, dear Renée.'

'It will grow again,' she replied, half
petulant, half soothed.

'And I have brought you this. It has
been blessed by the Pope himself,' he said,
kissing her, whereupon she clung to him
with a passion to which he tried to respond.

So the first storm passed, and the ill-
assorted pair turned into the courtyard,
where Mère Suzanne was sitting spinning
on the steps in the sun.

The deep sun-tinged rose-colour had returned to the young wife's cheek, her eyes looked purple, shadowed by thick black lashes, still wet with tears, so that Cecil forgot her dress for a moment in her beauty, and stood pensively admiring her while she showed her mother the gift he had brought her—a carved ebony rosary, linked with bright silver. He little thought then of the awful circumstances under which he would see that rosary again.

He did not remain long at St. Brileuc; he had his fortune to make, it was understood, and must go into the wide world for that excellent purpose. In the meantime Renée's education, at first at the hands of the parish priest, must begin; she must learn French and many things before going in the autumn to the school her husband would select for her.

Late autumn found him back in chambers preparing to go on circuit, and remembering that summer's experience as a dream. His mother had fulfilled her intention of going to the Pyrenees; he had joined her, and they had listened together for the echoes of Roland's horn, together roamed about in mountain solitudes, cork woods, and picturesque old towns, and also over those modern battle-fields so interesting to the General. Then the mother and son had some pleasant days of sunny leisure for lingering through the Alhambra, and re-peopling it in fancy to the music of its plashing fountains, while the General fled far away to Sadowa, averring that this freshly ensanguined field had as much of chivalry and far more of interest than Roncesvaux and forgotten Moorish battle-fields — an interest palpitating with the life of to-day and fraught with the destinies of the immediate future.

Yet these two imaginative people refused Sadowa, still ghastly from recent strife, for the Alhambra, hallowed by poetic echoes and fanciful adumbrations, read 'Le Dernier des Abencerrages,' sketched, and were happy. Lady Susan did not like to own even to herself that an indefinable quality she had hitherto found in Cecil was lacking. She had first felt the lack in his letters from Brittany; once or twice before she had been vexed by a certain reticence which amounted to a want of candour; there were painful moments in which she could not believe all that he said; she was absolutely certain that there was something studiously withheld from her in those latest Brittany letters. Most mothers feel the same in some degree, but—she had expected more of Cecil.

She pondered over it when he was at work again, making his first success as counsel for the defence in a murder case. It was as if a black curtain had been drawn between them. There were things in his mind to which she had no key—unexplained silences, melancholy broodings, an altered gaze in the eyes once so frank, some trouble that shrank from the light.

'I am not sure that Brittany was a success for you, after all,' she said one day in the Alhambra.

'It was not,' he replied ; 'the Celtic melancholy is not wholesome.   Invalids should go to Italy or Greece.   Even German fancy has more daylight cheerfulness than Celtic.   I stayed there too long, mooning over cromlechs.   I hate the place.   I'm sick of the very name.'

'Sudden likings, long loathings,' his mother said, and he looked up with a quick, questioning gaze, in a sort of guilty surprise that she observed with pain.

'At all events, he is brown and healthy,' she was thinking, 'and perhaps that horrid Georgie had more power over him than we supposed.   I hope her fine husband will beat her.'

The autumn circuit passed quickly and pleasantly for this promising junior, now

the laureate of the Bar mess, and filling
that onerous post with singular brilliance
and efficiency.

Bodily health being now completely re-
established, a flood of high spirits and a
rush of mental vigour naturally succeeded
it, and, as Cecil's friends affectionately
observed, he was in great form. His
young wife, in the meantime, was shut up
in a Parisian school, beating her wings
vainly against the bars, like some caged
wild creature. An exile in that foreign,
despised country, France ; bewildered by
the noise, stir, and glare of Paris ; constantly hampered and fretted by petty
restraints and conventions ; overstrained
by unaccustomed mental labour and deprived of the fresh air and manual toil
necessary to her health ; the laughing-
stock of silly school-girls, and, worst of
all, a victim to the wasting home-sickness
so keenly felt by the people of small and
unsophisticated countries—she was very
wretched.

She pined for the open sea and the great roar of autumn storms upon the rugged seaboard, pined for the breezy heaths, the country fare, the hum of spinning-wheels, and the burr of Breton voices and wail of Breton songs ; pined for the cows she had tended, for the smell of the hearth-fires and seaweed, the simple pleasant country ways, the solid square stone church ; but chiefly pined for her father and mother. She missed the enervating, fruity odour of crushed and half-rotten apples in cider presses and heaps under trees ; missed the robin's song, the smell of the first white frosts, the celebration of the *jour des morts;* longed for the absent husband of whom she had seen so little, and against whose decree of absence she sometimes fought with secret anger and bitter reproach. She began indignant letters to him and tore them up. She vowed to herself that she hated and scorned him who could leave her so lightly and in such misery. Then

again she melted into tenderness and sub-
mission, and delighted with the passion of
a mystic self-scourger in the very torments
she endured for this adored man. The
sedentary and confined life, which might
have ruined a less healthy and hardy
constitution than hers, produced a miserable bodily misease and constant dull
headache that made study still more toil-
some and unpalatable. This rendered
her irritable, and thus brought her into
humiliating disgrace. She sometimes
raged, sometimes wept, often prayed—on
the ebony rosary. But, on the whole, she
tried hard to learn and to prepare herself
to be a suitable wife to the husband who
had stooped to her. Perhaps people have
been canonized for less arduous denials
and strivings.

And after the notable day when she
threw three pupils in succession out of the
window—luckily, on the ground-floor—
she fared better in some respects, the
household having henceforth a wholesome

respect for the Bretonne's strong arms and
hot temper.   After all, life still held two
great joys—-one, her husband's occasional
letters, in the French she scarcely yet
understood, over which she knitted her
brows and tore her hair ; the other, his
precious gift, the ebony and silver rosary.

CHAPTER VIII.

THE LADY OF SWANBOURNE.

'PERMIT me, my dear Cynthia, to know best in this matter,' said Mr. Forde-Cusacke, with a slightly raised voice and in his most Parliamentary manner.

'By all means, papa,' she replied, with the demure set of feature which so often misled her stepfather; 'that is exactly what I wish you to do.'

The Forde-Cusacke family, with the exception of the antepenultimate Forde-Cusacke and the reigning baby, were at luncheon in a ground-floor room with mullioned windows which looked on a cedar-shadowed lawn. The windows were open, and a beautiful air, soft yet spark-

ling, and balmy with magnolia and other
flower scents, stole in, bearing the pleasant
intermittent sound of scythe on stone, the
croon of wood-pigeons, and the merry
defiant call of a cuckoo. Mrs. Forde-
Cusacke was looking reproachfully at her
second son, and was unconscious of anything else.

' Don't do that, Hugh,' she was saying
in a low, plaintive and exasperated tone,
which bore token of much repetition of
the phrase.

' I ain't doing it,' he returned poutingly.

' Then don't do it again,' she added
querulously, whereupon he made a face at
her.

' But,' continued Cynthia, not heeding
this interlude, the like of which usually
accompanied the family repasts, ' I am
afraid that you never will know better
until you have actually looked at those
cottages.'

' Sanders,' said Mr. Forde-Cusacke
magisterially, as he fixed his glass in his

eye to obtain a better view of his son's demeanour, 'have the goodness to remove Master Hugh from the table and place him on the largest oak coffer in the hall until he returns to himself.'

Sanders, whose clean-shaven face appeared incapable of the faintest shade of thought or emotion, silently proceeded to carry out this order, whereupon Master Hugh, in that spirit of pure devilry which sometimes takes possession of youth, suddenly wrenched himself from the man's hands, threw himself upon his back, and kicked.

'Sanders,' continued Mr. Forde-Cusacke, still looking through his eyeglass at the delinquent, whose ankles were promptly secured by a strong hand, 'have the goodness to lock Master Hugh in the oaken press until further orders.'

' Certainly, sir,' replied Sanders, vanishing with the wailing culprit.

Mr. Forde-Cusacke's eyeglass fell and

he addressed himself to his knife and fork
with an air of relief. This exercise of
domestic authority appeared to have a
soothing effect upon himself, as well as to
produce sudden and simultaneous good-
behaviour in all the little Forde-Cusackes;
yet he could not suppress a small sigh as
he regretted his inability to consign his
stepdaughter to the oaken press for the
next half-hour. He regretted it more
than ever when, after a few minutes' silent
reflection, she returned to the charge.

' Papa,' she said, ' I am convinced that
the moment you see those cottages, and
consider their condition when the brook
is full, the marshes flooded, or the mists
rising, you will say that the site is a mere
centre of diphtheria, and——'

' My love,' interrupted her stepfather,
with a suavity that boded mischief, ' I
must speak seriously to Clayton, and
request him not to distress and perplex
your mind with his professional fads and
fancies. A clever young practitioner, he

is naturally full of them, but he should know better than to thrust them upon the attention of young ladies.'

'It is not Dr. Clayton's opinion alone,' continued Cynthia; 'dear papa,' she added coaxingly, 'now will you drive over to Brooklands yourself with me——'

'My dear,' he interrupted with sudden resolution and unbated majesty, 'I will *not*.'

Cynthia knew when she was defeated and never wasted her strength in hopeless causes; she therefore dropped the subject. 'At least give me some more pudding,' she pleaded, 'though perhaps I don't deserve it any more than poor Hughie.'

'If he had only known what a stunner was coming!' murmured his brother.

Cynthia despatched her pudding with great enjoyment, while revolving schemes to prevent the repairing of those cottages in the marsh. They had been depopulated by last year's cholera, and were by this time quite unfit for habitation without extensive repairs involving considerable expense, which she considered might as well be applied to rebuilding them on a higher and healthier site, to which the old material might be easily transferred. This was no mere speculation on her part; she had thoroughly gone into the thing, and obtained a builder's estimate of the increased cost of her plan and its feasibility, besides discussing the sanitary question with the village doctor, who, being young, was still full of enthusiasm.

But if Cynthia was discreet enough to acquiesce in unavoidable defeat, Mr. Forde-Cusacke was far too good a general to neglect an opportunity of following up a victory, and, after a brief interval filled by the cuckoo's occasional mocking cry, the murmur of pigeons in the tall pines which served to blunt the fury of salt-sea winds and south-westerly gales, and

one long melodious warble from a blackbird in a lilac blooming near, he gave
his well-known preliminary cough and
began :

'Rome, my dear Cynthia, was not
built in a day, and it would be idle to
expect a young woman of years so unripe
as yours to have already acquired a full
comprehension of what is expected of a
woman, and especially of a minor, in the
singular position of possessing real estate.
That position, I need scarcely observe,
is as unsuitable as it is unusual for one of
your sex, a sex which nature has, for some
beneficent end, made incapable of——
Ah, hem !—that is to say, deprived of
the powers of—— Ahem !'

'Managing?' suggested Cynthia meekly,
without raising her eyes from the glass in
which she was attentively scrutinizing the
water-bubbles as they winked.

'Of possessing property in any real
sense.'

'Do you think *nature* did it, papa ?

continued Cynthia, emitting a spark from her suddenly-raised eyes.

'In so far as nature may be said to do anything, my love,' continued Mr. Forde-Cusacke, with an additional rasp in his unmelodious voice, 'it has made your sex incapable of owning property absolutely. Property left to a female is usually given in trust (as it always should be) to some male or males, on whom the duties and responsibilities attaching to such ownership are incumbent. As you advance in years and discretion you will see how unbecoming it is for women to arrogate to themselves any share in those affairs which properly pertain to men. As your guardian, I, and I alone, am responsible for the administration of your estate—both real and personal—until you are of full age. It is not for me to criticise your revered father's actions, but he was a very young man at his death, and probably had not fully considered the consequences of giving

the control of his property to a woman '
—-Mr. Brande had left his real estate
to his wife for life, with reversion to
his daughter, unless the wife married
again, in which event it went directly to
Cynthia—'else he would doubtless have
lengthened your minority and appointed
trustees.   It is possible that he took
it for granted that your marriage would
by that time have taken place — as,
indeed, I trust it will — when all responsibilities will devolve upon your
husband.   Pray do not concern yourself with cottages or building leases,
diphtheria or sea-side visitors.   Clayton
is an impertinent young donkey, as I
shall take an early opportunity of inform-
ing him.'

'Poor Dr. Clayton, to suffer for my
sins !'

'He is an excellent young man, Marmaduke,' Mrs. Cusacke interrupted ; ' and
what do we not owe him for his care
and skill in the whooping-cough ?'

'Nothing, my dear; I forwarded him a cheque for the amount at Christmas. But he is, as you say, excellent in his proper sphere, as Cynthia is in hers—if she would but keep to it.'

'Thank you, papa. But what *is* my sphere? I can't make puddings, because the cook would give warning if I did. People don't spin nowadays, and still-rooms are gone out.'

'Your sphere is that of your mother—marriage. Follow her example in all things, and you will do well,' replied Mr. Forde-Cusacke, rather hastily. 'By the way, Emily, shall you be able to give me an hour in the library this afternoon?'

An hour in the library meant the long golden spring afternoon spent in driest secretarial work, as Cynthia very well knew, and it made her heart ache for her mother, though this voluntary immolation was a privilege to that gentle and unselfish lady.

The prospect of following Mrs. Forde-Cusacke's example in all things was not enlivening to an ardent girl of nineteen, who felt her vitality in every fibre, and had dim forebodings of the fulness and beauty of life. Though she loved children—and a small fraternal hand was even now fondling one of hers—there was something appalling to her in the rapid succession of little brothers and sisters that she had witnessed for the last ten years ; their claims were so numerous and so imperative, and so often clashed with those of the head of the family, that the poor mother's existence seemed to her daughter to be swallowed up in them ; she seemed to live at high pressure in those lives, and scarcely had time to draw a breath, much less think a thought, of her own. This might be the highest life, but it was distressing to think of. Martyrdom is a fine thing, and asceticism compels respect; but——

So Cynthia mused with a chilled and

saddened heart, as she strolled out into the
sunshine, balked in her intention of carrying her mother off in a boat, with some
of the elder children, to a gipsy tea.
Nature was so joyous, and human life so
gray and grim. And yet all wives and
mothers were not extinguished and absorbed in this manner. Lady Susan
Marlowe, for instance. And hers, certainly, was not an ideal marriage from
Cynthia's point of view. Lady Susan
truly loved and admired her husband, but
she could only show one side of her manifold nature to that bluff soldier, who
was stone-blind to the others. Cynthia
even suspected that the General's conversation bored his wife. But, in spite
of occasional misgivings, youth always
cherishes the strange and pathetic illusion
—doubtless given by nature to prevent
the extinction of the species—that in
one's own case the ideal marriage must
come to pass ; others may make mis-
takes, but youth, sanguine youth, is sure

to choose well. The matter is both simple and inevitable, because one only falls in love with perfection.

Cynthia's spirits regained their native joyousness, while she walked in the blithe May day sunlight and tender tree-shadows. She turned and looked at the house, which was her own, and found it charming. It stood on a slight eminence, a moderate-sized building, originating in Tudor days, and altered and added to in various harmonious styles, so that it had the charm of constant unexpected-ness—an oriel here, a bay there, gable rising on gable, and dormer windows nestling in steep-tiled roofs. The warm old brick, of which it was chiefly built, was scarcely discernible on this southern side, on account of the greenery and bloom which climbed and clasped and smothered it, winding round the very chimneys, which were tall and twisted, and looking into windows, whence it was constantly being cut back.

The main entrance on the colder side
was less delightful to its owner.   In
spite of its fine Gothic porch and broad
flight of steps, people took their way in-
voluntarily to this warmer, homelier south
side, going in by the garden door or by
a long window of the little room on the
terrace, which, having no definite purpose,
served as a focus to which the life of the
house tended.   Here sprang the main
stem of the fine magnolia, the broad
leaves of which were shining in the afternoon sun; here the thick myrtle, and here
the rose, which, mingling with it and
withheld from blowing low down, sprang
in its joyous exuberance to the second-
floor windows.   Here stood out on the
turfed terrace a small turret, with a
tall tiled roof and gilt weathercock;
this turret Cynthia had from childhood
made her especial stronghold.   The trees
in the little park encroached too closely
upon the dwelling, adding to its woodland
and nest-like aspect; they were at this

season in their freshest green. Their
boughs grew low down and so luxuriantly
that, escaping from the shadow of the
cedar, the boughs of which swept the
turf, it was possible to lose one's self in a
moment in a maze of linden green.

The one defect of this charming nest,
its mistress thought, was an excess of
verdure and lack of flowers. But her
stepfather considered that more flowers
would involve a larger gardening staff,
and held that it was easier to lop green
boughs than to prevail upon them to
grow; further, that if, as Mrs. Forde-
Cusacke averred, Swanbourne was damp
in winter, it could easily be avoided at
that season. Melton, his place in Kent,
a brick barracks on a bleak hill, was
always dry, and more commodious for the
family. Swanbourne was, therefore, only
occasionally inhabited, to Cynthia's regret,
for she had lived there a happy child, a
little princess in her own right, until her
mother's second marriage, which occurred,

to her sorrow, in the ninth year of her
age. The family were now paying Swanbourne but a flying Whitsuntide visit,
moving, as that family usually did, solidly,
en masse, because Mrs. Forde-Cusacke
could not exist without the whole nursery
battalion, and Mr. Forde-Cusacke was lost
without his wife. Cynthia held views
upon second marriages which she could
not with propriety express in that
family.

'How I wish,' she thought to herself,
'that I didn't detest Mr. Forde-Cusacke
quite so much! I wonder how much he
hates me. I suppose it is as natural as
caring for one's own parents. There will
be an explosion some day, when he is a
little too selfish and tyrannical to mother.
I suppose I shall say things. It will be
a pity, because we should have to part.
But it would do him good.'

She had penetrated the bowery gloom
of the lindens, which merged in a wild
copse, sweet with the scent of young

leaves, and carpeted with hyacinths. It was hateful to think of her mother shut up indefinitely in a stuffy library, doing dry secretarial work. Hugh would be a better boy among the hyacinths than mewed up in the oak-press; the other children were in the schoolroom; she alone was free. So she went a little sadly through green lanes and meadows, and far up the steep face of a down, to a thorn hedge, whence she could see nearly the whole of her small domain.

Here the air was very sweet and sparkling, and the sounds delightful. The drowsy, contented murmur of pigeons in wind-bent pines sheltering the greener woods, whence came an intermittent nightingale gurgle, scarcely distinguished from the daring attempts of an ambitious blackbird intoxicated by the spring; now and again from the heart of blossomed chestnuts the joyous, irrepressible self-assertion of the cuckoo; overhead the clear, celestial melody of larks and solemn

cawing of rooks ; and all round her, what
was inexpressibly dear to Cynthia, the low,
hoarse, continuous booming of the long
sea-waves as they broke unseen in perpetual surf at the base of high cliffs on the
seaward side of the down.   Once on this
down-top, you had a peaceful inland prospect of woodland, meadow, and homestead,
with a village and a square gray tower.
The sea, thundering at the pillars that up-
bore the turfy slope on which she reclined,
was invisible to Cynthia, whose gaze was
fixed upon the condemned cottages which
her quick eye saw far-off in the marsh.

The sight of them spoilt the spring
music, because her mental gaze saw children
sickening, and men and women wasting
from poisonous exhalations within them, so
she turned to her right.   There the long
ridge of down suddenly sloped to the sea-
level, its cliffs curving inland and forming
one horn of a tiny azure bay, the other
horn of which she could not see.   The
bit of bay was so land-locked, as seen

through a stile in the hedge, that, but
for its white surf-streak, it might have
been a lake. There a row of bent pines
half concealed a collection of slate roofs ;
this was Seagate, the little watering-place
the sudden up-springing of which on
her father's land was the chief source
of her wealth. The sight of this, too,
vexed her. Shortly before her father's
death certain plots of his land had been
sold on building leases. Hence a ghastly
row of jerry-built stucco villas, a focus of
cheap-trippers, bathing-machines, nigger
bands and other horrors. The evil of
those stucco villas was irremediable, besides
being a source of income ; but another
plot of land offered in her father's time
was now about to be taken to build more
such villas. She did not want more
building, but, if it were inevitable, wished
at least some restriction on the manner of
it. Further cheap and nasty building
meant the extinction of the special charm
of Swanbourne.

If the building could only be delayed till she was of age—two mortal years—or till her marriage, then she would stipulate that the houses should be properly built. Then she would give a certain piece of land for a little church, which the sudden growth of Seagate had made necessary—a free church, in which the poor should be made especially welcome and comfortable.

Her stepfather said she would have to leave such things to her husband. But, of course, her husband would do exactly as she wished, she reflected, with a little smile, dimly recalling the protestations of various rejected suitors. Yet was she, indeed, an irresponsible being, and her life a mere fraction of another's? Was marriage in sober truth mental and moral suicide, life-long suttee? Good people said so, but good people had often piously burnt each other for slight differences of opinion.

Strong life leapt through her veins,

dim unrealized affections and unawakened
instincts throbbed in her heart, many
thoughts surged in her brain, latent
capacities struggled for development there
—was all this purposeless and futile?
She seemed to have no duties beyond
dressing well and being charming and
well-bred. Her fine raiment and dainty
and luxurious surroundings came chiefly
from the land she saw before her, yet
she might not lift a finger to prevent
people being poisoned upon it. Well,
the advent of the ideal lover would set
everything right.

That ideal fairy prince! Merely to
think of him in the May-day sunshine was
bliss. No actual happiness approaches that
of this visionary Eden of maiden youth.
Marriage at nineteen means the blissful
union of two equal and cognate, yet diverse,
souls, expressly created for each other,
and incapable of living apart; each supply-
ing the other's need in a sweet partition
of joy and sorrow, each with absolute

trust and devotion, mutual reverence and
delight in the other.   Just as surely as
the white may-bloom turns to red fruit,
this union in maiden fancy will take
place.

Cynthia had often pictured and loved
this chosen man in day-dream, as Brito-
martis saw and loved her destined knight
in Merlin's magic crystal. Many virtues he
would have, with a few charming defects
to set them off.   Above all, he would be
as unlike Mr. Forde-Cusacke as possible.
That poor gentleman's defects were,
indeed, not charming ; his very virtues
had an unpleasant flavour. It must be
confessed that as a companion he was
impossible.   He possessed a singular
power of diffusing an atmosphere of dis-
comfort about him ; while his impervious-
ness to humour made him perfectly irresistible as an object for subtle sarcasm.
But, though the worthy man was selfish
and tyrannous in his family, he was not
so much more so than others as Cynthia

supposed. It must be granted that he had a hard and unsympathetic judge in his step-daughter.

No such fairy prince as Cynthia dreamed of had as yet been discoverable; still, she knew that in due time he would come. She would then have definite duties, the chief of which would be to adore and be adored by this beatific man ; ·he would unravel the tangled mysteries of life for her—hand in hand they would travel heavenwards. Just at the right moment that perfect knight would come. But he never comes.

She was looking at the dark pine tops traced on the blue bay, their trunks concealed by a fold of ground, her eyes deep with these guileless visions, when a dark figure suddenly eclipsed the soft azure, and, passing swiftly over the turf and the stile, alighted with a thud exactly in front of her.

It was that of a young man, rather tall,

and strongly made, with a brown, slightly
aquiline face, clean-shaven except for a
small whisker, a broad forehead swept by
a wave of thick, dark hair, and dark eyes
full of intellect. In his surprise he had
snatched off his straw hat, and she at
once recognised him from his photograph
as her friend's favourite son, Cecil
Marlowe.

CHAPTER IX.

ON BOTH SIDES OF THE SEA.

It was possible to know Cynthia Brande
long without discovering the singular
beauty of her eyes, because it was only
in moments of deep emotion or intense
thought that their unusual charm was re-
vealed. At such moments the pupils
expanded until the iris became a narrow
rim of which the original colour was lost
and replaced by glow-worm green scintil-
lations; they were indescribably beautiful thus kindled. Of those eyes, and the
young, unstained, ardent soul gazing from
them, Cecil was aware and of nothing
else, during those few intense moments
into which a life-time seemed crowded.

Afterwards he had a vague impression of
a white gown, a straw hat like an Eton
boy's, a spray of may-blossom in the belt,
and a general atmosphere of youth, grace,
and purity.

Cynthia, thus surprised in maiden
meditation, was a little taken aback, and
turned very pink in the mingling of
dream and reality. Then she rose, the
pinkness fading, and the intense light
leaving her eyes, as she smiled and spoke,
her words chiming with his.

'It must be $\begin{cases} \text{Cecil Marlowe !'} \\ \text{Cynthia Brande !'} \end{cases}$

She was glad to see him, and said so
cordially, giving him her hand frankly—a
bare, warm young hand, the honest clasp
of which might have cheered a Timon of
Athens—remembering that she was on her
own ground and so bound to welcome her
guest. Then the strangeness of the unexpected meeting wore off, and they
strolled on over the flower-braided turf,
exchanging suitable commonplaces—one

of them seeing the fresh-leaved woods, calm sea, and blue unclouded sky in a new aspect, and thinking some subtle change had passed into the manifold music of earth, sea, and sky.

When Cynthia rose, a small plainly-bound green book slipped from the folds of her dress. Marlowe picked it up; and they had reached the summit of the down, looked at the shadowy ships sailing in the offing and at the fringe of sea-thrift growing along the verge of the cliff, pure pink traced on pure blue, before he looked at the volume and read its title, 'Daffodil Songs.'

'Oh, Miss Brande!' he exclaimed, flushing darkly, 'what a sad waste of time!'

'I like them,' she replied, also flushing, but with the colour of the sea-pinks; 'I should like some more such daffodils.'

'Oh, but even real daffodils only come in March; when there is nothing else people put up with them—and east winds,' he said, turning the leaves and seeing, with a smouldering glow of pleasure in his eyes, pencil-marks, comments, and dates in the margin.

'Nobody has any idea,' he said, 'what a rise in life it is to find that people actually read one's rubbish.'

'I never read rubbish,' she corrected, with severity, 'much less mark it. Daffodils may blow only in March, but May lilies and June roses follow, Mr. Marlowe.'

'So do thistles and stinging-nettles and that charming flower scenting the woods I passed to-day—wild garlic,' he added; and then it seemed time to explain that, having so often been prevented from calling at Swanbourne, and finding no immediate prospect of doing so otherwise, he had walked from Cottesloe to the bay in the forenoon, and was now just on his way to the house.

'How strange,' he said in conclusion. 'that we have not met since you were quite a little girl in short frocks!'

'Dreadfully afraid of you as a grown-up Oxford man.'

'Yet I dare say we have often been in different corners of the same houses during these last weeks. Once I had a back view of you riding ; my mother pointed you out. She speaks so often of you.'

'And of you to me. It is a great thing for me that Lady Susan lets me be her friend—an education in itself.'

'Perhaps it is a greater thing for my mother. Women need daughters ; they keep them young.'

'I suppose when people are growing old they wish to be young,' Cynthia said pensively ; 'they forget what a trial youth was when they had it.'

'Youth a trial ? What can be said against youth ? This is quite a new notion.'

'Youth is so helpless ; it is so ignorant, and has not found its level ; and then,' added Cynthia, turning a little to look at her fever-stricken cottages, 'it has not bought its experience.'

'Ah!'

Cynthia was a little surprised by the deep-chested sighing monosyllable, uttering which, Cecil looked with a cloudy, abstracted gaze over the little bay and beyond a line of warm red cliff, capped with bluish green and bordered with white surf, behind which cliff rose the fine outline of an amethyst-coloured hill, dreamy with air-magic, and running in broken contours far beyond the red cliff-line gradually down into the sea, where a sheet of foam on the azure marked a dangerous reef.

'Experience may be a fine thing,' he added in a harsh voice ; ' but it's always too late by the time it's bought. It can only be made into good advice, which nobody will have.'

' Only tell me where experience is sold by the ounce, and I will buy it at any price,' she replied, with an acidity that seemed foreign to her.

He turned again, and was facing the

Breton coast ; he was glad when he had completely turned so as to face Cynthia and have Brittany well behind him. There she stood in her simple girlish dress, still counting her years by teens, able to have all that money can buy, leading the safe, sheltered life of an English girl, admired, caressed, and courted, yet perplexed, sensible of something amiss in this incomprehensible world, in which she might naturally revel with the unthinking gaiety of a kitten, and desiring to buy the bitter fruit of experience. And there was a flight of pale-blue butterflies hovering over the short down flowers in the sun. ' Be like the butterflies, graceful symbols of mirth, and don't think,' was his first thought ; then something in her face touched him.

' Heaven send you never buy your experience !' he exclaimed, looking at the pearly buds of the may in her dress, and identifying them with herself. ' And whatever you do, never marry out of pity,' he added impulsively. Then, after an embarrassed pause on both sides, 'That is only a bit of slang,' he said ; 'the tag of a silly song. A certain set of us use it as a warning not to do anything in a hurry.'

Cynthia was a little taken aback.

'Oh,' she replied, laughing, 'I hope I am not so foolish as that. Marrying out of pity is next to murder.'

Then they walked on as if to make up for lost time. How foolish to loiter in this lazy fashion ! Here was Mr. Marlowe on his way to call on her mother; the afternoon was passing while she chattered in this absurdly outspoken way. Perhaps he thought her an empty-headed little fool. *He* was no fool. Then of a sudden the image of the dream-husband, chased away by Cecil's presence, returned and made her blush. The dream-husband now cut but a poor figure ; she even suspected him of being a prig and a donkey. As for Mr. Marlowe, there was something in him she did not quite like ; she was not clear what it was. Perhaps he was too clever; she had always been a little afraid of Lady Susan's clever son. After all, those foolish youths who fell head over ears in love with one, and had not the sense to veil their feelings, were amusing in their way and not unpleasant for an hour. Perhaps Mr. Marlowe's keen dark eyes, so like and yet so unlike her friend's, saw too much. What if they had divined her dreams—those foolish girl-dreams? She turned hot and hotter at the remembrance of them. What a sentimental idiot he would think her! Perhaps Lady Susan's accounts of her had bored him, and also shown her to him in all her native foolishness and ignorance. Well, he might think as he pleased; it was nothing to her.

Yet, though she hurried on, it took long to reach the house. There were so many charming glimpses at every turn—glimpses of sea especially—and this inquisitive Mr. Marlowe wanted to know the name of every bay and headland and the exact position of every lighthouse; he seemed to think her a walking Murray.

'There can be nothing between that point and America,' he said, pointing westward with his stick.

'Only air, sea, the earth's roundness, and probably a few ships,' she replied, with a caustic accent, which struck him as out of harmony with her.

'Do you know what you are looking at now?' she asked, when he faced about and left America to its fate.

'Surely I am looking at you for the moment.'

'For the moment. But a country of magic and marvel is behind me. You are now looking straight into—Brittany.'

He started, his countenance changing; then he looked searchingly, yet almost furtively, at her, turned and walked on.

Cynthia was pursuing her way at a sedate pace, to which civility obliged him

to accommodate his own, while the perpetual plunge of the hidden sea on the
rocks below asserted itself almost to the
exclusion of thought.

The beauty of autumn inspires a peaceful, dreamy content ; that of spring pierces
deeper and arouses vague, vast, consuming
desire, which the Germans name *Sehnsucht*—a word beside which *longing* is pale
and ineffectual—but which is something
more than even *Sehnsucht*, restless yet inspiriting, fretting yet vitalizing, the birth-
pang of new life. If we die daily, we are
also daily being born. Thus in springtime
we, like all living things, throb and thrill
with a vital impulse we cannot fully obey ;
hence strife, which is pain, and, according
to Goethe, salvation.

Perhaps it was this spring influence—
émoi d'avril—which filled Cynthia with
the vague, boding sadness she felt in herself, and saw in Cecil's face during the
long silence which followed her allusion to
Brittany.

A turn in the linden alleys presently revealed a detachment of Forde-Cusacke infantry, and little boys and girls came running up, open-armed, with cries of :

' Cynthia !'   ' Here is Cyn !'

A very small one was hoisted up to Marlowe's shoulder, and so borne to the house, while others clung about Cynthia's skirts.

The day was too pleasant for indoors ; Mrs. Forde-Cusacke took the sunshade and shawl her daughter brought her and went out under the cedars to receive Cecil. Mr. Forde-Cusacke, with many inward groans, emerged from his library and correspondence, and they all sat in the shade and talked and drank tea.

The shadows slanted, bees hummed in fruit-blossoms, the sky grew more liquid, the sunshine more golden, swallows began their nightly revel and the fluting of blackbirds took on the heart-piercing mournfulness of evening ; it was one of those delicious hours, like those occasionally peeping out of childhood, that people remember all their lives. Some people might have wearied of the monologue of which, when he had a good listener, Mr. Forde-Cusacke's conversation chiefly consisted; his strictures on Mr. Gladstone and the disestablishment of the Irish Church might have been delivered in a less rasping and monotonous voice, but for Cecil the evening was too divine to be spoilt by trifles, and he could think quite comfortably while agreeing with Mr. Forde-Cusacke, who, poor gentleman, preferred being disagreed with to a certain extent.

What a lucky fellow Dick is! was the chief burden of Cecil's reflections as he watched Cynthia's white-clad figure moving about among teacups and children scattered on the grass, and heard her occasional laugh or brief speech. Why had he not seen her before the Phyllis episode? Would it have been any good? Probably not. Then Dick had to be considered. Happy Dick!

'I think this is yours, Mr. Marlowe ; Marmie picked it up by the meadow gate,' Cynthia said, approaching him during a pause in the Irish Church.

He was looking at a may-tree covered with white blossom and steeped in yellow sunlight till it seemed to glow of itself, like an Alpine snowpeak after sunset. He turned at the sound of her voice to take a foreign letter inscribed with his name in a careful, unformed handwriting, at the sight of which his heart turned to stone.   The lustre died from the sunlight, the enchantment left the magnolia perfume, Mr. Forde-Cusacke's pomposity suddenly became oppressive, and Cecil remembered that he could scarcely reach home in time for dinner, even if he started at once. Cynthia, clothed in spotless white, with her young, clear-eyed gaze, was like an accusing angel forcing upon him what he could not remember without acute pain, his wife's last letter.

That same live warm sunshine sparkled

on the Channel waves, and gilded the sails
and burnished the hulls of many a vessel
tacking over them ; it was lying with even
deeper brilliance on the rocky Breton coast,
and making the orchards glow redly.   And
there, at that moment, looking with
wistful eyes across the Channel towards
England, sat, beneath the crimson canopy
of an apple-tree, the writer of the letter,
thinking of her husband and planning
another letter, while she hushed the
young baby in her arms.

Cecil bent his way homewards with
rapid strides, which, had they been as
swift as lightning, could not have out-
stripped the haunting cares pursuing him.
Does folly bring more misery in its train
than sin ?   Why, in heaven's name, had
he done that thing ?   Was it pure pity ?
Then it was vain ; Renée would have
been unhappy if he had left her, but not
so unhappy as now.   He was miserable
near her, and yet he could not be happy
long away from her ; she haunted him

with the corroding misery of an accusing
conscience.   There was no way out of it,
and his wife—it had come to this, that
he almost regretted it—was incapable of
giving him any excuse for separation.
Well, he would do his duty ; when she
was sufficiently educated, she must be
brought home and presented to his people;
it would be cruel to bring the untaught
girl yet into the midst of foreigners and
strangers of a rank so far removed from
hers.   She must at least speak decent
French, if not English.   He would be
good to her—oh yes !

In the meantime, it would be better to
keep it quiet.   Why distress his friends
needlessly ?   Unseen troubles do not exist.
Who could tell what might happen ?
Life is uncertain.   She had been at the
point of death that spring.   How tell his
mother he had married a wife he could
not introduce to her ?   No, no, she must
be educated first.   And then, after all,
how few marriages are congenial, yet

people put up with each other, living their own lives apart beneath the same roof.

So he thought upon this side of the sea, while upon the other the home-sickness, pining, and beating against bars like a wild caged creature, together with the perpetual alternation between fits of fury and fits of penitence, had brought poor Madame Cecil to such a pass during her first winter in Paris that she had to be sent home to save her life when the spring days came.

Once in Brittany, the first breath of the salt, live air of home revived her, and she gradually regained strength and spirit among her own people, until upon this beautiful May day her face had as deep a bloom as the crimson cider-apple flowers beneath which she sat, singing to her five-weeks-old baby :

> * ‘ They were affianced, a youthful pair ;
> In youth, alas ! they divided were.

° From Archbishop Trench s translation.

'Two fair babes she has brought to light,
A boy and a girl, both snowy white.

'"What shall now for thee be done,
Who hast brought me this longed-for son?

'"Shall I fetch thee fowl from the sedgy mere,
Or strike in the woodlands the flying deer?"

'"Wild-deer's flesh would please me best,
Yet wherefore go in the far forest?"'

The girl was evidently not worth thought or thanks. Why was this tiny Cécile one of the unfortunate sex? Yet to the mother the little unconscious thing was sweeter and lovelier in some respects than a boy-baby would have been. But who wants girls? And what do they bring but their own sorrow? Cecil might have taken pride in a son, and perhaps wished to see him, and so left his business to come to her. He had actually seen his daughter, aged one day, crimson, crumpled, wide-mouthed, and loudly bewailing her unsolicited and unwelcomed entrance upon this planet. She had inspired him with mingled terror and disgust.

But Père Michel and his sons gladly welcomed the new daughter of their house, chirped to her, snapped their fingers at her, and handled her with skill and appreciation, being accustomed to babies as part of the usual furniture of life.

The bees hummed in the apple-blossom above Renée's head, covered once more by the white cap ; the blue sea quieted more and more in the evening peace ; the baby slept on, and the mother, with the aid of a dictionary lying on the grass, painfully composed a wonderful letter in English, her first in that tongue. ' The eyes of thy daughter is shoeblacks,' it said, which surprised her husband until he read further on that the child was soon to wear her first pair of ' sloes,' and that her first words were to be spoken in English.

However stormy our lot may be, troubling or troubled, we all begin life in this peaceful fashion, rocked upon the heart of a woman. Nero smiled in such infantile repose as this girl-baby's, so Homer smiled and Plato and Caligula, Isaiah and Iscariot, the murderer who was hanged yesterday and the judge who sentenced him.   And the mother who hushed each baby to his rest knew little as this young wife for what tragedy or glory she had borne her child.

CHAPTER X.

'WELL, since you ask me, Dick,' Cecil said, looking straight before him and speaking in a voice of studied indifference, 'she is simply the most charming girl I ever met.'

The guests were gone, the household had broken up for the night, and the brothers repaired to the cosy smoking-room at Cottesloe Grange for a chat and a cigar. The Forde-Cusackes and their daughter had come in the afternoon to a large garden-party, and the ladies had remained to dine, Mr. Forde-Cusacke passing on to a political meeting in the next town at which he was due. Thus

Cecil had had ample opportunity for improving his acquaintance with Miss Brande, of seeing her under various aspects, and especially of observing the marked yet unobtrusive attention that Richard Marlowe paid her. Happy Richard, free and able to offer homage at any shrine that attracted him !

Though he had never (except during the brief delirium of the imagination inspired by Georgie Vivian, the Phyllis of the verses) had the slightest desire to pay such homage, this freedom seemed to Cecil, chafing in his fetters, the most blessed thing in life, worth almost any sacrifice to obtain or preserve. Unluckily, he had not valued that blessedness until he lost it.

'If it wasn't for that infernal money of hers !' sighed Richard, pulling cruelly at his fair moustache.

'Well, but, after all, Swanbourne is a very little place.'

'Ah ! but old Brande made piles of

money in lucky speculations; nearly all
Seagate is hers as well. And, except for
her mother's share, she gets it all at
twenty-one; she's no end of an heiress,
confound it!'

'There's nothing very confounding in
marrying an heiress. You'd be a precious
deal more confounded with a penniless
wife, Dick.'

'A fellow in a line regiment, with little
more than double his pay, is no match for
an heiress, Will. And, besides my not
having cheek enough, she may think I
want her money; and I only want her,'
he added plaintively.

'My good fellow, every time you look
at her you tell your story. Go in and
win! Is the poor girl to be doomed
to single blessedness because she's an
heiress?'

'Then she's so awfully clever. And
I'm not exactly a genius, you know.'

'Now, Dick, did I ever accuse you of
it? You know how to choose a wife, and

that's about the luckiest gift a man can have. You inherit it from the General. Go in and win, man ! go in and win !'

' To be sure,' Richard replied, brightening, ' the General chose a clever woman, and it turned out well. But, after all, if he hasn't the brains the mother has, the dear old man is clever in his way. There's not a finer officer in the service. It's an awful shame he should be on the Retired List.'

' True—very true. He distinguished himself greatly in the Crimea. How we boys use to gloat over the war news ! And in the Mutiny, too. And he was mentioned in despatches. Follow the example of that dear old man, Dick, and receive my paternal blessing. Marry——'

A cushion, neatly aimed at his head, and as neatly dodged, stopped the speaker's eloquence, and hit the majestic butler, who was just coming in with a tray of glasses, in the face, after which it subsided with a crash in the tray.

' What's all this ?' cried a jovial voice behind, as the General followed in. ' Marry, indeed ! do nothing of the kind, lads, and then you won't have a couple of long-legged sons turning your smoking-room into a bear-garden.'

' Don't mind him, sir ; it's only his play,' Richard apologized. ' He is often taken like this.'

' But when you do,' added the General, after the door closed on the butler, 'choose a girl like Cynthia Brande.'

' What, both at once ?' asked Cecil.

' One at a time, Cecil. Dick is the senior ; let him have his innings first. When he's bowled out you go in.'

' Thank you, sir. Play up, Dick. By the way, isn't there to be a match to-morrow ?' Cecil asked, wishing to change the subject.

' There might be, if Dick could bring himself to the point,' replied the General, chuckling at his own wit. ' I've often wished one of you had been a girl, boys ;

though, if you had, you wouldn't have been equal to Cynthia, after all.   Amy is a nice girl, and suits Harry to a T; but she's a stranger.   Now, I've known Cynthia all her life, and liked her.   She's thrown away on that pompous ass, Forde-Cusacke.   The girl is good and sound to the backbone.   Ask your mother; women understand women.   Your mother is a remarkable woman, boys; what brains you have you get from her.   And Cynthia is quite up to her mark; see how they hit it off together.   And, mind you, girls in these days are not always well-bred; they are loud and fast.   Now, Cynthia is a thoroughly well-bred one.'

'Rather!' echoed Dick.

'And well-born,' added his father. 'There was a Brande at Hastings.'

'So I always understood,' returned Cecil; 'but the arrows seem to have done most of the business there.   Then there was the brand Excalibur; but those battles were prehistoric——'

'What the deuce is the boy talking about? Now, there is nothing I hate more than marrying beneath one,' continued the General. 'A woman always shows her birth in one way or another. Besides, it comes out in the children. It's bound to.'

Cecil stooped to flick some cigar-ash from his coat, and this of course made him turn red. 'Ah, people don't think much of that sort of thing in these democratic days,' he murmured confusedly, when he was once more upright.

'More's the pity! Everything is going to the dogs. Especially the services. No, no, Cecil; don't ask me to receive an underbred daughter-in-law and a tribe of plebeian grandchildren,' he added in an aggrieved and angry tone.

'My dear sir!' cried Richard, laughing. 'Has Cecil merited this aspersion? Did he ever show symptoms of such a disease?'

'I can't stand midnight cigars more than twice running,' cried Cecil, jumping up. 'I envy fellows who can. Good-night.'

'That's the worst of those clever fellows,' his father commented when he was gone. 'Cecil has no more nerve than a cat. He looks as seedy as the deuce. And only one mild cigar and a glass of Vichy! Pass the cognac, Dick.'

'Poor old chap! He's not been the same man since that illness,' Richard said. 'That was Georgie Vivian's doing. He was hard hit there.'

'Your mother swears it wasn't Georgie Vivian, but overwork. You fellows don't know how to fall in love in these days. Why, the first time your dear mother refused me I'd a good mind to blow my brains out.'

'She couldn't have had you if you had, you see,' said Richard thoughtfully.

'So I thought; besides, there was no pistol handy, and it happened to be Derby Day. It would have been a pity to miss that year's Derby. I lost a pot of money, and the Lord only knows how I got home. I always fancied some fellow put me in the body of his drag and delivered me right side uppermost.'

In spite of the sweet country air and sweet country quiet, Cecil could not sleep that night; he tossed about and thought over the day's events, simple and tranquil as they seemed to be. Why had he always put off meeting Cynthia Brande: was it an instinct of self-preservation, or had he seen through his mother's thinly-veiled desires respecting her? It was an irreparable mistake; to have seen her earlier would have spared him the fever of that fantastic love episode, not to mention the graver folly that ensued in Brittany. He would have liked to wipe that little country out of the map of Europe and memory, instead of which it haunted him day and night. He could not, especially with these new claims on his purse, afford to let such rich material for copy as his Breton experiences furnished go to waste. A series of Breton sketches, appearing in a periodical, had been recently collected, illustrated from his own drawings, and made into a charming little volume, now lying conspicuously on a drawing-room table, and offering material for after-dinner conversation.

'And you say you do not like Brittany or the Bretons, Mr. Marlowe,' Cynthia had objected that evening ; 'and yet you describe them so charmingly and make your readers like them.'

'Perhaps I saw too much of them,' he replied, 'so the glamour wore off.'

'There is nothing so hateful as an old love,' his mother commented. 'Cecil, I had no idea you were so fickle. See this wedding picture, Cynthia ; it is a perfect idyl. Can one believe in such things in this prosaic age ?'

'Did this picturesque wedding really take place only last year ?' Cynthia asked, looking up at him with her direct smiling gaze ; 'and were you actually present, or did you dream it all ?'

'I took an unimportant part in it,' he

replied gloomily. 'That of bridegroom,' he added to himself.

'Quite like the old age, is it not?' his mother went on in her enthusiastic way. 'This gavotte under the trees is too delightful. But of all the Breton pictures, I like the Corregan best.'

And there on the wall, her eyes following Cecil with a perpetual reproach, wherever he turned, hung the finished water-colour sketch of his wife, as he first saw her. The fact that his mother had so often seen and discussed the picture made it daily more difficult to tell the tale. She had found it lying forgotten amongst others in his portfolio, and at once singled it out as the gem of the collection, and he could not refuse to let her have it.

'That Corregan is a forward young party,' Richard commented; 'the moment she sees a fellow she proposes to him, and looks him to death if he won't have her. It gives one the creeps to think of it.'

'Oh, but that is only the fairy, Captain

Marlowe,' Cynthia objected ; 'masculine spite against our sex invented all those wicked Lorelei myths. This is a real flesh-and-blood girl, whom your brother actually knew ; did you not, Mr. Marlowe? —I dare say she is a good, hard-working, honest girl in reality; a little rough, no doubt.'

'Living hard, suffering often, wholesomely stupid and *bornée*, and perhaps by this time married to a cruel husband,' added Lady Susan, contemplating it through her uplifted glasses.

'Her eyes are wonderful,' continued Cynthia, who was standing fascinated before the picture ; 'what does she see with that intent, startled gaze ? Is it Life? or is it Destiny? The poor, pretty bare feet!—there is a sort of pathos about them ; the thorns of life must so often wound them. And the symbolic burden!'

'The Breton women have awfully hard lines,' said Richard, while Cecil turned away. 'Don't look any more, Miss

Brande ; that girl will give you the blues as she does me. The sight of her future husband ought to be enough to make a French peasant girl look glum. My brother should call it, " The First Sight of the Future." The French call their husbands " futures " before they are married.'

' And presents on the wedding-day, I suppose ?' rejoined Cynthia, turning from the picture with sudden relief.

' And wish they were pasts six months after, no doubt. Miss Brande, won't you sing our blues away ?'

So Cynthia sang Richard into paradise, but she did not sing the pain out of Cecil's heart. And why must she sing ' Huntingtower' ?

> ' " I dinna ken how that may be, Jeanie,
> I dinna ken how that may be, lassie,
> For I've a wife and bairnies three,
> And I'm nae sure how ye'd agree, lassie."

> ' " Ye should ha tellt me that in time, Jamie,
> Ye should ha tellt me that lang syne, laddie,
> For had I kent o' your fause heart,
> Ye ne'er had gotten mine, laddie." '

'Listen!' said Lady Susan when the song was over—'the whole of the third generation lifting up its voice in one fell cry!'

'The little beggar has fine lungs,' added the General, as the voice of his year-old grandson was heard pealing from a distant nursery at the opening of a door, and Mrs. Harry Marlowe hurriedly left the room to investigate the matter. 'The little chap will make his way in the world and take his own part.'

'I had hoped there was an end of him for the night,' grumbled Richard; 'that blessed infant is always being handed round, as if he was coffee or liqueurs. It's hard lines on you, Mrs. Cusacke, with so much of that kind of thing at home.'

· 'Our first and only grandchild, Dick!' expostulated his mother, 'and we are not all bachelors, remember.'

'Nobody pities the sorrows of oppressed uncles,' Richard complained. 'I feel for that poor fellow in the " Babes in the Wood." What he must have gone through at the hands of their grandmothers and mothers and lady friends !'

' And pray who gives the child surreptitious sweets and rides on his shoulder?' asked Cynthia. ' Not Uncle Cecil, but Uncle Dick.'

' I confess that I like babies at a distance best,' Cecil replied, thus challenged, while Richard said something about the duty of kindness to animals.

Parallels between the antepenultimate Forde-Cusacke and the hope of the Marlowes here ensued, and it was agreed that the latter had the finest legs, though, perhaps, the former used his with the greater vigour, while Cecil broke an ivory paper-knife to pieces.

A sort of rage consumed him. He was forced mentally to see the same kind of thing going on in the ruined château in Brittany, with his child instead of Harry's as the centre. Harry's wife reminded him of Renée when she bent over the little boy—the same look was in her eyes, the same clipped baby-talk on her lips, the same cooing sound in her voice.   There was the same delight of grandparents exulting over the first baby: Mère Suzanne, instead of Lady Susan, offering the domestic idol a metal spoon, instead of a gold watch; the same haughty toleration of worship on the part of each dimpled divinity.   There were the young uncles, too.

The simple dark Breton interior, the women spinning, Renée rocking the wooden cradle with her foot, the hearth-light reflected in the panels of carved oaken coffers and press beds, the hum of the wheel and the harsh Celtic voices, pierced often by the child's wailing, strings of sausages and onions depend-ing from the rafters, the wooden rack that held the spoons, the indescribable mingling of odours, over which at this hour bad strong tobacco usually rose triumphant — no nursery for the little girl Marlowe; there is neither reticence nor concealment in peasants' homes — what a contrast to this English home, with its soft lights, fresh flower scents, pictures, books, and various harmonious adornments, the softer, mellower tones that are heard in the voices of cultivated people, their gentler speech and manner! Picturesque, unwashed, superstitious Père Michel shared his grandchild with the handsome old soldier clad in fresh linen and well-cut dress suit. Cecil's mother and his sister-in-law in laces and silks, with white hands and delicate faces, Lady Susan's instinct with intellect, and touched with the indescribable quality that belongs to birth and breeding—what a contrast to the Breton mother and grandmother!

And all the evening long Renée's face on the wall was looking at them all with those haunting, reproachful eyes, discussed, patronized, even pitied. And some day they would have to see her, and know what she was to them.

Busy as he now began to be in his profession, Cecil's social instincts were strong, and he found time to be in society a good deal after the spring circuit. And now chance turned in the other direction, and he began to meet Cynthia wherever he went as persistently as he had hitherto missed her. Richard was often in town at that time as well, and Cecil grew more and more accustomed to look upon him as her destined husband.

But one bright summer morning the quiet of his chambers was broken by the entrance of Richard, debonair, erect and handsome as usual, but with a curious gleam in his eyes that made his brother ask him what was up.

'I'm going to exchange into an India bound regiment,' he replied.

'Don't do anything in a hurry, Dick.'

'I've done it. The game is up. What's the good of humbugging about when a girl talks like that? Honour—friendship —regret—didn't know what a fellow was driving at, and that kind of thing. Hang it, Will, you needn't pull a face a yard long.'

'You don't know what I would give to see you married to Cynthia Brande,' he burst out. 'Don't go abroad, Dick. Try again. How many times was the General refused?'

'Oftener than I shall ever ask. Mother told me I'd no chance from the first. Besides, it isn't fair to hang about a girl like that. It keeps off more suitable men.'

'Oh, Dick, this is quixotism—pure quixotism. No better fellow than you will ask her. And no man will ever care, even for her, more than you do.'

'That's true enough,' Richard replied thoughtfully; 'but then, you see, she likes some other fellow better.'

PART II

CHAPTER I.

LOST IN A MIST.

SUMMER came and faded, winter blustered by and softened into another spring ; the may blossomed white and blushed pink once more, and was followed by the wild rose, and now the hawthorns were covered with dark-red berries and the glory of September lay like a blessing on the resting earth, to which robins sang their cheery lullaby.

The sweet-water grape ripened out of doors that fine autumn ; it was already swelling in abundant clusters on many a sunny garden-wall and homely house-

front ; orchards were unusually fruitful
and pleasant to see ; late roses bloomed
freely ; as yet the Swanbourne woods had
not begun to turn, though the Virginia
creeper blazed to the chimney-tops of a
thatched cottage in the village, wrapping
it in a crimson network seen from afar.

Stubble was still stubble in those days ;
gleaners still found it worth while to
break their backs over harvest fields,
while the cottage was shut for the day
and the cradle and youngest children were
placed in safety under the hedge with
the day's provision of cold tea, bread and
cheese, and apple turnovers. Women
and children told each other how much
they had 'leased' that year in comparison with the last, and rural life had
one more picturesque and pleasant feature ;
for, if the leasers' backs ached cruelly, their
lungs took in noble supplies of sunny air,
and they enjoyed the change and social
chat of a long, though laborious, picnic at
the most suitable time of the year.

Birds were plentiful and well nourished in that year ; men and dogs invaded the shining stubble-fields, and every now and then the sharp crack of guns on the warm, still air, and blue curls of smoke over hedges hung with gossamer, proclaimed the end of all things to certain partridges.

'And they were so happy this morning,' Cynthia Brande said.

She was sitting under the cedar where the ladies had been having tea and talk ; the shooting-party had just returned and were showing their spoils : piles of limp bunches of brown feathers with piteously dangling necks and patches of blood were strewn on the sward at her feet.

'Thou canst not say I did it,' Cecil Marlowe replied, sweeping the birds away with a smile ; 'if Mr. Copley made the biggest bag, I can safely boast that I made the biggest misses.'

'I absolve you,' Cynthia said with a smile. 'And I admire Mr. Copley's skill

—but I wish the poor birds were alive again.'

'So do I,' added Lady Susan. 'It is illogical, because I like game.'

'I fear that I, too, appreciate the poor birds at table,' Cynthia confessed ; 'but the idea of killing these pretty harmless creatures, who enjoy their life and liberty, makes one miserable.'

'Be comforted, Miss Brande,' returned the ruddy young sportsman addressed as Mr. Copley ; 'men still exist who carry guns through turnip-fields all day long expressly to save partridges' lives.'

'Men may carry guns for a worse purpose, Mr. Copley,' replied Cynthia, with a cold severity that warmed Cecil's heart, and made Mr. Copley say wicked things to his own moustache.

'After all,' interposed Cecil, 'anyone who has had a bad toothache has suffered more by long odds in half an hour than any bird bagged to-day.'

'A clean shot is the easiest death

going,' added Mr. Copley: 'just a hot sting and there you are !'

'There you are no more, you mean,' Cecil murmured.

'When will you give up making bad puns?' asked his mother. 'Those little limp bunches of feathers possessed that intangible and inexplicable quality called life this morning. They breathed, moved and felt. Some little lead pellets struck them : they became motionless, breathless, senseless matter. It may not be very hard to feel a moment's pain and then feel no more for ever.'

'But they *wanted* to live,' objected Cynthia, with moist and brilliant eyes. 'And then the wounded birds, who crept away to die by slow torture !'

She looked at Cecil as she spoke, remembering that he had told her once that he was no sportsman, and only shot for exercise and good-fellowship, that he was weak enough to be almost incapable of killing anything, though he saw the

inconsistency of his position and its dis-
harmony with the general plan of pitiless
yet pitiful Nature.

'I cannot kill a rabbit, yet I would
gladly shoot some human beast who kicks
women and little children to death,' he
had once said ; ' when I was a boy I once
heard a wounded hare squeal; and I never
got over it.'

' And I,' Cynthia had replied on that
occasion, ' when I was a little girl, heard
my pony shriek because it had staked
itself, and saw them shoot it out of pity.
I could not forget it : I fell ill ; they had
to take me away for change of scene.'

Cynthia's look at Cecil, who was
leaning against a tree hard by, was met
by one of those long, involuntary and
magnetic glances that form epochs in life ;
it was observed by Mr. Copley with a
sudden disclosure of the whites of the
eyes, such as is seen in a vicious horse.

'*Sportsmen* don't wound birds, they
kill them clean,' he said savagely ; ' the

wounding is done by the duffers who miss.'

He did not rise in Miss Brande's estimation by this remark. She turned and looked at him with a cold and haughty surprise that made him grind his nice white teeth. He was a well-built, well-featured lad of the blue-eyed, yellow-haired, conventional English type, and though so coldly eyed by the lady of his affections, he made as he stood at ease, slightly leaning on his gun, in cartridge-belt and gaiters, with his felt hat pushed a little way off his strong, broad, stubborn forehead, a figure that most ladies might contemplate at least with toleration, if not with pleasure.

' Really ?' she returned icily. ' I should have imagined that those who hit birds were more likely to wound them than those who miss.'

' My dear, Mr. Copley is quite right,' interposed Mrs. Forde-Cusacke, in alarmed haste, while Cecil passed his hand over his mouth to conceal a smile, and looked down, seeing nothing but the edges of Cynthia's dress trailing on the sunny turf.

' My dear mother,' returned Cynthia, with a smiling sweetness that was too good to be real, ' we all know that Mr. Copley is a crack shot and thorough sportsman. I did but venture a mild supposition as an ignorant and unlearned person. He knows,' with a winning smile, as she glanced up at the unfortunate young man, ' that I would not presume to have an opinion on a subject so strikingly his own.'

Mr. Copley's blue eyes gleamed and his nice white teeth became slightly visible at this. ' Of course one doesn't expect *ladies*,' he graciously observed, with an emphasis calculated to wither Cecil, at whom he glanced acidly from the tail of his eye, ' to understand sport. I hate women who shoot. Lots of them do nowadays. They make the jimmiest little guns for ladies. I couldn't marry a woman who stumped over the stubbles with men all day popping at partridges,' he added, with the exquisite modesty that prompts the average male to make his own requirements in a wife the ideal standard of the sex.

'That is just as well,' Cynthia observed reflectively, gazing into such distance as the linden growth admitted, ' because,' she added, with a green scintillation in her suddenly raised and as suddenly lowered eyes, ' you see, you couldn't marry us *all*, now, could you ?'

'All ? Good Lord, no !' he returned, happily unconscious of a delighted grin on his rival's face ; ' I should be quite content with—with—with——' Here the poor youth suddenly blushed crimson and stammered.

'With one—just the flower and pearl of her sex ?' suggested Cynthia, with an artless and maternal sweetness. ' May you win her, dear Mr. Copley, in due time ! What *has* become of Marmie ? I wonder if you would mind seeing if he has parted with his beloved gun ? The mere sight of a gun intoxicates the boy.'

'Delighted,' murmured the misguided youth, hurrying off to fulfil his mission.

'Would you like a stroll down to the bay, Lady Susan ? There will be just time before dinner, and the sunset will be brilliant. The children are all on the sands, mamma, and we can bring them back, you know.'

'Charming !' from Lady Susan, and 'Delightful !' from Mrs. Forde-Cusacke, and the group on the lawn moved off in the opposite direction to that taken by Mr. Copley.

Cecil paused one moment before accompanying them. 'It is a blackguardly thing,' he thought, remembering Dick's 'It isn't fair to hang about a girl and keep other men away.' And Dick had a right to pay his addresses to her. He might have won her. And this young

Copley was a suitable match. Their lands adjoined, his family was good, he was strong in the domestic virtues. Then he reflected that Mr. Copley, as well as the General and himself, was to dine at Swanbourne, and might, if so minded, as public report affirmed he was, pursue his wooing later on. He also reflected that a man who had passed the whole day in the constant and imminent peril to life and limb, involved by Mr. Forde-Cusacke's proximity at a shooting-party, was entitled to some indulgence by way of compensation.

'I've been through a good many campaigns,' the General observed that night, 'and come out of a good many smart engagements, but I'll be ' — something military—' if I shall come with a whole skin out of another day's shooting with Forde-Cusacke.' That day, however, the only unintentional additions to the good gentleman's bag were a dog, the General's coat-tails, and a beater's hat—rather a costly item this, since, as the worthy beater remarked, ' 'Taint only the hat I looks at ; it's what anybody med look to find inside of en.'

Therefore Cecil walked through the little park and over the shoulder of turfy down to the bay with momentary lightness of heart, the little party straggling and grouping itself, dividing and reuniting with the exigencies of the path, but chiefly with Cynthia and Lady Susan in the van, and himself in the rear with Mrs. Forde-Cusacke, whom he was entertaining with some amusing conversation. This, however, was not so absorbing as to prevent him from ruminating on the hint Marmaduke had let fall in crossing a turnip-field that morning, to the effect that George Copley was ' gone on ' Cynthia, that he was no end of a good fellow, and that he earnestly hoped she would have him. The boy would not talk in that strain unless matters had gone far, he thought.

Nor was Marmie's hint the only one. In the heat of the day he had turned aside, sick of the uncongenial sport, and lain under a hedgerow-oak to drowse and dream in the sunny noon. Then voices from the other side of the hedge, where some gleaners were dining under the shade of the same broad and hospitable oak, fell half-heeded on his drowsy ears.

'A bushel o' vlour comes handy, I hreckon, Mis' Brown, but 'tes ter'ble hard to come by,' said a female voice, indistinct from bread and bacon. 'Billy, my dear, hreach me the cwold tay, wull ee ?'

'Zure 'nough, Mis' 'Ood,' replied another homely voice ; 'but there, I 'lows every little helps, if it do pretty nigh break anybody's back in two.—You, Jim, you wun't get nar a mossel o' vittles without ye minds what I sez to ee.'

' The vield work I done when a gal was wuss,' said another ; ' 'twus like a hred-hot hay-fark drawed in and out o' any-body's lines. 'Taint ooman's work ; men

doos it nowadays. Times was haerd in
my young days, I 'lows.'

'Times med a ben haerd, but they
wusn't so ter'ble dull. There was more
weddens they times, and there was more
dooens at they weddens, no michen off
like a wold fawkes after vowls to a hregis-
ter, but prapper Christened weddens in
church ; bells a-hringen, and ale and cake,
and all sorts. Vokes wusn't ashamed o'
holy matterimony they days, so there
wusn't so many gals gwine hrong.' Here
a young mother coloured, and tried to
seem unconscious of certain looks and
nudging of elbows.

'Weddens! I 'lows there's weddens
anuff and to spare. Wold Tom Larkins
a-marryen that there zimple young zote,
Liza White, a Tuesday! Wold chap had
the bells hrung too.'

'Then, ther's our young lady up Swanbourne and young Squire Capley. I 'lows
that'll be a zight to zee.'

'Ay, and there'll be dooens at Swanbourne, I'll war'nt, Mis' 'Ood. — Em'ly, you young vaggot, you stop acten and mind the baby, wull ee ?   I'll gie ye a clap on the chaps, ye bad mayde !—Our young lady is open-handed and pleasant-spoke. Many a good turn she've a-done we.'

'And we, too, Mis' Brown. The Lard knows what I should a-done without she when my master went off Wold chap always wus ter'ble slow, slow at his coorten, slow at his vittles ; but, Lard a massey! when it come to dyen, I thought the poor wold chap never would a-done wi't, a was that slow with his dyen. There ee bid a bed vive martial months, and me with a babe at the breast, let alone vour bigger uns, and him a dyen day and night all they months and nothen but what I yarned meself, and the parish.'

'Iss,' piped a thin old voice, ''twill be a vine wedden ; young Squire Capley's a prapper man, straight in's back and strong on's legs, steps out like a man, a doo, and Missie, she've a vaäce like they pink swate paes down our Jim's and a voice like a drush's.'

' There'll be coals give out, I'll war'nt.'

' Ter'ble nigh to Christmas, 'tes. The Lard send the wedden a goodish time aforehand. — Now then, young Jarge, you give me the baby, and take and goo an a-lazin'. You can ate that there apple while you pecks up carn, I 'lows.'

Thus the matter had been discussed as a settled thing, and there were many speculations as to which house would be chosen by the wedded pair to live in. Copley Hall was larger and more commodious, but Swanbourne was so pretty.

The scene on the lawn made Cecil doubt the certainty of that match. Cynthia had too acidly resented Mr. Copley's sarcasms, though, of course, it might be only a lovers' quarrel or a girl's coquetry, fighting off the final but inevitable surrender.

Nor did Cecil's conversation with Mrs. Forde-Cusacke prevent him from thinking of his wife's last letter, praying him to let her come to him, and representing that England was the best place in which to acquire an English accent and manner. It need not be an expense to him, she urged ; she and the child could live very well in his chambers ; she would do the *ménage*, and wash and mend for him, thus saving him a servant. She could now read English, and might help him in writing and many other ways, she bid him consider ; besides, absence and loneliness were breaking her heart, even though she would be allowed to take her child back to school with her that autumn.

Cecil felt that the thing must now be done at all hazards. He must provide a suitable home in or near London, of a size warranted by his professional income, which was rapidly rising, and was considerably augmented by literary work. About Christmas he would explode this shell in the family, introducing the little girl, if it should prove a desirable and

well-mannered child, first, thus awaking
an interest that he feared Renée would
not herself inspire. If the General with-
drew his allowance, he could do without
it; if his favour, that would be unfortunate; his mother he was sure of, in any
case. No doubt there were many worse-
assorted matches than this, and yet men
lived and did men's work in spite of them.
He must give up society; his home
would be wretched; he must lie on the
bed his own hands had prepared : but
home, after all, is only a small fraction of
a man's life; club life, and the fun and good-
fellowship of the circuit bar would still
be his—his profession offered increasingly
brilliant prospects, besides being of absorbing interest. The worst thing in the
business would be his father and mother's
vexation and disappointment. Not quite
the worst thing, after all, for there would
always be a vivid sense of what was missed
and might have been but for that hasty
marriage. Other men might have formed

a less binding but less honourable tie in place of this hasty marriage, a moral impossibility here—a tie which, even if it had existed, would have bound him as strongly as this.

But he could still meet Cynthia and continue to enjoy the fellowship that had sprung up between them ; it might ripen into a real and lasting friendship, and no harm done ; yet how perfect a marriage might have been between natures so congenial ! She would marry ' that lout Copley,' to think of whom made Cecil sympathize with Hoël Calloc.

' Well,

> ' " So one day more am I deified—
>   Who knows but the world may end to-night ?" '

That brief sunset hour should at least be his.

The eastern horn of the bay was rosered, as if burning in pale crimson fire; pale lilac tints shadowed the western horn ; behind it blazed splendours of autumnal sunset, tingeing the white surf at their

feet purple and red. They lingered a few
minutes in the bay, and then set their
faces towards the west, intending to walk
along the sands, a thing possible only
when the tide was low, and, climbing a
winding path that led up the cliff from a
little cove, to return by that way to Swanbourne. Mrs. Forde-Cusacke and Lady
Susan were much occupied with the elder
children, who had joined them, so it was
natural for Cynthia to walk with Cecil.

But the children lingered on the sands,
dragging their elders with them, so Cecil
and Cynthia took another turn on the
sea-wall, silent, listening to the wild cries
of many a solitary sea-bird, the soft,
rhythmic boom of the surf, and the gentle,
leisurely explosion of long rollers, broken
on jutting buttresses of rock, and thus
sent flying upwards in foam-wreaths dyed
in sunset.

> ' What need to strive with a life awry ?
> We ride together, breathe and ride.'

They did not observe that the firm level

sea-rim, darkening against the pale salmon colour of the lucid sky, had softened into a silvery haze before which the sea was paling more and more, and which was trailing in flaky folds over the nearer waters.

'See,' Cynthia said presently, pointing to a cormorant sitting dark, and motionless as a halcyon, on the tranquil sea a little way off shore, 'how harmless it looks, rising and falling, as the waves roll under it, like a ship at anchor! But it is not peacefully meditating; it is watching sharply for some poor creature to eat for its supper.'

'How do you know he is not lost in contemplating the mysteries of the universe, like those Thibetan monks? At the worst the old fellow is helping to keep the proper balance of animal life in the sea. Can you call that harm?'

The morality of the cormorant's proceedings led to all sorts of questions and insoluble problems, until a cold damp shiver warned them that they were wrapped in mist, through which objects loomed with dim, distorted outlines and exaggerated bulk.

'Only a sea-fog,' Cynthia said, looking at the thin mist-shapes rolling in at the base of the down like a procession of ghostly giants.

'You will be wet through and get a bad cold,' grumbled Cecil.

'Oh, it is often like this in the bay— why, where are the others?—and clear and sunshiny on the down. I dare say it is perfectly clear at Swanbourne.'

There was nothing to do but to hurry on, Cecil rather dubious as to their whereabouts, but trusting in the topographical knowledge of the lady of the manor, who trusted in the same.

The conversation now naturally turned on the Niflungs, who proved as interesting as the cormorant, and as absorbing, while behind the partial mist-folds the pageant of sunset slowly blazed itself into a golden glow on the far west waves, filling the broad moon, now slowly lifting herself above the eastern waters, with red fire. Meanwhile the surf lines crept nearer and nearer the tall cliffs, on the bases of which they would dash themselves long before full tide.   Presently Cynthia stopped, descending like a shot bird from some airy cloud-summit of speculation.

'Mr. Marlowe, we have passed the turn up the cliff!' she cried.

This was too evident ; and, moreover, the mist had rolled inland, leaving the sea clear, so that, beyond the rocky corners they had turned, they saw only a wide sheet of churning surf, gleaming with the intense whiteness that comes after sunset.

'And the tide running strongly in,' added Cecil, inwardly cursing his own stupidity.

'Well, Mr. Marlowe, our only chance now is to round the next point before the tide covers it,' said Cynthia tranquilly.

They hurried on, the tide coming in with sudden plunges that drove them up into the furthest bend of the cove.

' Run, if you can without stumbling,'
Cecil cried, quickening his pace, 'on my
arm, Miss Brande—on my arm, and
hold on for your life if you slip.'

' We shall do it, never fear,' she replied,
running—' hand-in-hand, that's safer.'

The cliffs, eaten out at their bases by
the continual action of the sea, rose some
hundred feet sheer above them. The
whole sea seemed to be plunging into the
cove at once, a great roller broke white
over the rocky jut they had to climb
before they could reach the deepest curve
of the cliff-wall, where the tide rarely
climbed. Cecil looked at Cynthia with a
singular expression. He did not think
they could possibly round the rocky spur.
This would effectually solve all his diffi-
culties.

' Beware of the tenth wave, Virgil's
wave,' cried Cynthia as they ran. 'We
shall do it, never fear.'

On they sped hand in hand over the
wet shingle, over the slippery rocks, still

foam-spattered from the last great wave,
Cecil on the sea side, his feet washed by
the surf of each advancing wave, which he
counted with a beating heart up to the
eighth, and then his nailed shooting boots
slipped on the oozy stone, and he would
have gone under and certainly been swept
off by the fatal tenth wave before he
could get up again, but that Cynthia's
slender hand closed as with a grip of
steel upon his, and her wrist suddenly
became rigid as iron, giving him the exact
support necessary to recover his footing.
Then the ninth wave plunged solidly
upon the rocks, drenching them with its
spray, just washing Cynthia's feet and
covering Cecil over the knees, and they
bounded on to the shingle and landed
above high - water mark in a narrow
chasm, just in time to see the mighty
tenth roller dash itself breast-high on the
face of the cliff.

They stood facing each other, Cecil
holding Cynthia's hands in his.

' Cynthia !' he cried, with an indescribable accent, ' Cynthia !' His dark eyes
blazed, his lips were set as if in wild
endeavour to keep something back.
Cynthia was agitated, too ; her eyes
overflowed with the marvellous light
they shed at times ; her hands ached in
the strong and desperate clasp of Cecil's,
which left them white and cramped, yet
she scarcely felt it.

' I was frightened,' she said, with a
little catch in her voice.

' Frightened ! You nearly let me drag
you under ; you held me up—you, with
these small, small hands.'

' Just a turn of the wrist one learns in
riding. Very easy,' she replied, with-
drawing her hands. ' Yes, I was desperately frightened, Mr. Marlowe, for we
were only just in time, and the rocks
were slippery.'

' *I* was desperately frightened. I didn't
know what pluck you had,' he said, looking
at the white plunging rollers, dashed into

flying foam by the jutting cliffs, and seething broadly on the shingly cove up to their very feet.

Cynthia looked with the fascination and awe inspired by elemental forces on the great white army rolling in, crest after crest, with incessant deep-mouthed roar, in the magical light of dusk and moonrise. 'See how peaceful the sea is beyond the surf, and the moon so calm!' she said, pointing to the pathway of quivering golden scales the just-risen moon was making on the waters; 'it would have been just as sweet and peaceful if we had been lying beneath.'

'Would to heaven *I* were!' he thought.

'I am like my little sister, Daisy,' she continued, smiling with moist eyes and slightly quivering lips. 'She is the family prodigy, you know. "Oh, mammie!" she said this morning, "I *shall* be so sowwy when I is dead and can't have no more bekfasts, and no more wocking-horse, and no more birfdays, and no more nuffing."'

CHAPTER II.

THERE stood Cynthia, conspicuous in her white dress against the gray cliff towering three or four hundred feet above her, in the magic light of mingled sunset and moonrise, her eyes sparkling, her cheeks flushed, speaking of the joy in life natural to youth, a creature instinct with the charm of young vitality, touching in her very joyousness, and but just snatched from death.

Cecil looked at her in a kind of madness, all his nature stirring and seething —gently at first like the golden sparkles of moonlight on the waters, then deeply, broadly and fiercely, like the wide white surging of the ever-crashing rollers at the cliff-base. Wave after wave of tumultuous emotion rushed over him, sweeping reason and conscience away, dashing him on rocks of pain, bewildering, blinding, deafening him.

He turned, looking seawards, still as any stone, away to the farthest amethystine headland, on the extreme point of which a bright star flashed out, faded, and flashed out again from the unseen lighthouse tower.

He knew his liability to sudden and dangerous fits of strong feeling ; one such storm aroused by Hoël Calloc's brutality in contrast with Renée Kérouac's beauty and helplessness was the first cause of his unlucky marriage. Another had urged him to fight the tipsy tinker for the possession of an ill-treated boy, now his devoted friend and servant. But this storm threatened graver issues.

He dared not look at Cynthia ; had she spoken just then it would have been all over with him ; but she was silent, absorbed in thought.

The mellow thunder of plunging waves, the scream of the back-draught as it tore the shingle away, steadied his nerves; they drowned slighter sounds and made her quick breathing inaudible. If he could but shut her out of his thoughts, forget that he might have won her, might even now win her with one word !

He tried to think of the wooden cradle and its crying occupant by the glowing hearth on the other side of those heaving surges, of his slighted young wife's loyalty and devotion, of what he owed to her and also to the innocent girl at his side.

In the meantime, Cynthia's quick breathing gradually quieted, and her musings came to an end. But Cecil's silent inward struggle was long; it became oppressive to Cynthia, who was magnetically influenced and disquieted by it ; she grew uneasy : his looks were strange, his face pale and unusual, his mouth rigid.

The ever-recurrent crash of shingle, dragged down by the ground-swell, contained an endless menace to him, a sound to haunt him for years in dreams.

'What is the matter?' she asked presently, growing more uneasy; 'were you hurt when you slipped on the rocks?'

'No,' he replied, looking straight before him. 'I was only wondering how to get you out of this scrape. The tide is not yet full, and it is a spring tide. It will be hours before it will be possible to go back by the shore.'

Then the ghastly possibility of having to pass half the night there occurred to them. They must get out of the bay; yet to be isolated together there in the face of Nature's unadorned magnificence, cut off from the pettiness of everyday life, their ears filled with the infinite longing of that restless surging sea glimmering in the magic of mellow moonlight, was perilously charming. Madness came once more upon Cecil; he was consumed with desire to snatch the slim white figure in his arms and plunge with it beneath the snowy surf-sheet, where they would lie clasped together for ever in the green depths of the sea. Wild words were on his lips, his blood throbbed in his ears, when Cynthia suddenly steadied him by pointing to some unevennesses in the side of their chasm, by clinging to which it was just possible to climb to a kind of rocky stair or chain of detached footholds, winding along and up the cliff face, and often used by egg and samphire gatherers. Her head was steady and her footing sure ; he, as she knew, had ascended the Eiger that summer.

'Though it would be pleasanter to stay here,' she added, 'but for one thing.'

'It would indeed,' he echoed, wondering that she was unconscious of his madness, 'but for one thing. But what is your one thing ?' he asked quickly, thinking of George Copley with a deadly pang of jealousy.

'Need you ask? when we dine at eight and it must be at least half-past. Think of them all at home! Our cook makes the loveliest mayonnaise. And then her savouries! That happy cormorant! he has only to turn upside down to get his dinner out of the sea. Fortunate creature!'

So she could jest and trifle, while his soul was rent asunder and his heart tortured to death. His eyes blazed; he could have hurled her into the sea. Dinner meant George Copley, his ruddy face rising like a harvest moon above an expanse of white shirt, as blank as his blundering mind, his stupid blue eyes devouring Cynthia while he absorbed savouries and sweets, soup and side dishes. Well, she should be kept no longer than he could help from Mr. Copley's brilliant and delightful society. He could have borne to lose her; but the thought of 'that lout Copley' having her was hot acid poured on an open wound.

The children had given their sister some toy reins to carry; they were long and made of stout braid; these he knotted together for a guide-rope, too short to be used in the proper way. He tied one end firmly round Cynthia's wrist over a wad of handkerchief to prevent cutting; the other end he fastened to a strongly clasped leather belt he was wearing.

'This is quite an adventure,' Cynthia said, while the rope was being fitted; 'almost as bad as your night on the rocks off the Brittany coast. Did you ever find out who had been playing tricks with your boat, Mr. Marlowe?'

'Oh, that is a long story and very tedious. Don't let yourself slip if you can help it; the jerk would wrench your arm —seriously perhaps. Cry out when your footing slides or you lose your head, and I will hold you up. Luckily, the lowest part is the worst, if we should come to grief.'

He had tried the first climb and found

it practicable, and, the night being
windless, except for a light breeze off the
sea, and almost as bright as day, from the
harvest moonlight striking full on the cliff
face, the ascent was effected with only
one serious slip on Cynthia's part, which
not only tested the rope's strength and
Cecil's steadiness, but sprained her wrist.
She regained her foothold quickly, yet
slowly enough for it to seem an age to
him before he could reach her with his
hand.   And when at last they stood side
by side on the smooth moonlit sward that
sloped seawards, their heads dizzied by the
frightened birds screaming and circling in
eddying flight from the cliff beneath, and
heard the surf booming in hushed cadence
far below, he was in his right mind,
having been gradually sobered since the
shock of Cynthia's wholesome prose.

'You are very brave,' he said quietly.
'You would enjoy a hard snow mountain.
But that last quarter of an hour was bad.
It was touch and go with you.'

She was gasping with exertion, pain and hunger, and perhaps something more potent still. She felt as if a good cry would have done her good, though why, she could not tell. She was glad to take the hand he offered, for the short turf was dangerously slippery, and so they climbed to the top of the down. The touch of her tired clinging hand went to his heart, with the beauty of the night, into which some pale stars had trembled, and the peace of the shining sea and silvered woods ; he could not bear to think that they would soon be divided for ever. It had been well if the sea had swept them into its shimmering depths, never to part again.

They walked silently and swiftly homewards over the dewy turf, Cynthia soon lagging, too tired to keep up the pace. Yet Cecil did not offer her his arm.

'You are tired,' he said, 'take my stick. It was as good as an alpenstock to-night.' So they went on again in the pleasant silence, which was broken only by the continual soft under-song of the surf below until Cecil again spoke.

'Miss Brande,' he said, 'I think I may congratulate you, may I not?'

'Of course you may,' she replied indifferently.

Her words were like a knell; it was true, then. He tried to say some of the usual commonplaces, but his lips were stiff and dry.

'But congratulate me on what?' she added, roused to a languid interest by his silence.

'I beg your pardon if I am premature. It is generally known—Mr. Copley——'

'Mr. Copley indeed! Were you thinking of that nonsense? I wonder they don't select some more probable creature to gossip about. Oh, you don't know Swanbourne, Mr. Marlowe. I believe I was engaged to a coastguardsman last Christmas.'

His heart bounded, his temples

throbbed ; he wished he had not asked ;
he was too glad.

'This kind of tittle-tattle is most
irritating,' Cynthia continued tranquilly.
' Even if he had any such intentions, Mr.
Copley is far too sensible not to see that
there could never be anything of the kind.
We are old friends, as you know, and
I have the greatest regard for him.'

He strode silently on beneath the pale-
lavender sky, which was dotted with
sparse silver stars, occasionally slackening
his pace to let her weary steps keep up
with his, but never offering his arm or
observing that she held her bruised and
sprained wrist in her hand. 'She must
know all, and I must see her no more,' he
was thinking, as he stared moodily down
on the moonlit turf.

Cynthia had received much homage,
both true and false, such as naturally falls
to young and pretty heiresses. She knew
well how to conduct these affairs—to
gently stifle false hopes and avert crises

with tact and kindness ; she thought, too, that she was able to diagnose such maladies of the heart with accuracy. But this sufferer exhibited such perplexing symptoms. She was piqued ; she had given him his lead, and he had not followed it. Had she been mistaken in her diagnosis, had she let him see too much in her false certainty, had he dared—actually dared to play with her ? She turned crimson at the thought. Yet the symptoms were too spontaneous, too restrained, not to be real.

She thought it singular that what softens and refines rude and coarse men should make this one brusque and almost uncivil. ' We are walking,' she thought, ' like a tramp and his wife, except that he doesn't actually swear at or strike me.'

He had not spoken for so long that the silence, together with the ghostly gleam of the moonlit chalk-cliff, the magic and mystery, and soft sound of the sea, with the consciousness of vital emotions at fullest tension between them, was more than she could bear, and her lips quivered in spite of herself.

'Confess honestly, Mr. Marlowe,' she said at last, in her gayest voice, though she was never more inclined to cry, 'that the thing you most long for at the present moment is something to eat.'

'I will honestly confess, Miss Brande,' he replied gravely, encouraged by the unconcern with which she spoke, 'that the thing I most long for at the present moment is the courage to tell you something that is on my mind.'

'Speech is free,' she returned airily.

'Speech *is* free, but not to cowards. What I have to say is very serious, and —should have been said—before—when first—— Oh, I ought never to have seen you! But I could not help it. I was under a spell, and did not know it. The charm grew and grew—I was like a dreamer.'

There was a shrill cry of 'Cynthia!'

the sound of a small figure alighting on the turf before them, and Marmaduke cleared a gap in a thorn-hedge near. He seemed like a small impersonation of destiny, snatching Cecil's last opportunity from him.

'Why, here you are at last! Where *have* you been? Mother is as frightened as she can be. Me and Simmons started to look for you. He's gone the other way. The governor said you couldn't have come to grief with Cecil to look after you,' Marmaduke began breathlessly, and Cynthia, utterly upset, was glad that the adventure was at an end.

In a very short time Cecil, duly fed and dressed, went into the drawing-room, and had to account for himself under the fire of many eyes.

'Ah, well, we have all been young, and all lost ourselves once,' Mr. Forde-Cusacke observed, with his usual happy knack of blandly blundering upon excruciating topics.

George Copley glared at the new-comer with looks sharper than carving-knives and the corners of Lady Susan's mouth twitched. To Cecil's horror, the Willoughbys, who had entertained him on their yacht off the French coast three years ago, were present, the *Firefly* having put in at a port a few miles off. Who could tell what they might have heard, or where they might have been in Brittany?

Cynthia's entrance quickly followed, and her appearance and demeanour, though he dared not risk more than one rapid glance, reassured him.

Plainly dressed in black velvet, with a single row of pearls round her throat, her hair as simply and as swiftly coiled as possible, she was quite composed and serene, though her eyes were unusually full of light. She had not seen the Willoughbys before, but made no apology for her late appearance.

' So glad you were able to come !' he heard her say, as she approached Mrs.

Willoughby in such a manner that the intervening furniture made it impossible to shake hands and thus call attention to her sprained arm. 'Yes, Mr. Copley, these sea-fogs are most confusing, and they come up so rapidly—picturesque, though damping. This one portends fine weather—does it not, Mr. Willoughby?'

'I hope so, because Mrs. Cusacke has promised for you that you will spend the day on board the *Firefly* to-morrow.'

'If you have made no other engagement in the meantime,' Mrs. Willoughby added rather cruelly.

'No, I have made none ; to-morrow is perfectly free, dear Mrs. Willoughby. I shall be delighted. I shall never forget those delicious evenings on deck last summer. Too tired to sing ? Oh no ! And must it be " Huntingtower " again ?'

This little ballad was one especially suited to Cynthia's voice, and the dramatic way in which she gave it made it a favourite with her friends. To-night,

being very tired, she had to make an effort
to sing, consequently she excelled herself,
particularly in the pathetic parts.

> ' " I dinna ken how that may be, Jeanie,
> I dinna ken how that can be, lassie,
> For I've a wife and bairnies three,
> And I'm nae sure how ye'd agree, lassie," '

she sang with a humour that seemed
ghastly to Cecil ; then followed :

> ' " Ye should ha telt me that in time, Jamie,
> Ye should ha telt me that lang syne, laddie," '

with a rising pathos that made him feel
as if his heart would break.

> ' " For had I kent o' your fause heart " —

indignantly—

> ' " Ye ne'er had gotten mine, laddie," '

with gentle heartbreak.

Poor George Copley saw that Cecil
was much moved by the song he believed
that Cynthia was singing so well for ' that
fellow's sake.' He sat glowering at both
and savagely gripping one of his own silken
ankles, listening and meditating some
terrific and annihilating sarcasm upon his

fortunate rival.   But he was a better
marksman with the gun than the tongue,
and when he marched up to Cynthia to say
good-night he ended with this fulmination :

'Do you think, after all, that shooting
partridges is a more cruel sport than getting a woman hanged ?'

Cynthia looked blankly surprised ; then,
following Mr. Copley's glance at Cecil,
who was close by, smiled condescendingly
at the mild satire.   Then she remembered
hearing Cecil wonder how judges could
endure the emotional strain of criminal
courts, when even to be counsel for prosecution in capital cases was so trying.

'One gets hardened to many things,' he
had said ; 'but to put on the black cap
must need nerves of adamant and a heart
of steel.'

Yet quite recently he had been one of
the prosecution in a notorious case in
which a murderess was found guilty, as
everyone present knew.

Remembering that, she wished Mr.

Copley a chilling good-night, and turned to Mr. Willoughby, who was talking about a fatal accident which had just occurred in France. She listened with an undercurrent of thought on Cecil's hatred of war, his sympathy with the Buddhist principle of never taking life, and his consequent futile attempts at vegetarianism. Was he, after all, but a sentimentalist? Had his mother's natural blindness infected her and cast a glamour over an amiable, but weak character?

'It was in the evening papers,' Mr. Willoughby was saying; 'the church was crammed, chiefly with women, some festival being held—processions, with any amount of lighted tapers and flimsy banners. Immense loss of life. But these things are always exaggerated.'

'Mostly women, of course, poor things!' Cecil said languidly. 'Did you say near Orleans?' with sudden interest.

'Yes, certainly, Orleans. I forget the name of the place. A panic did the mis-

chief, as usual.—Then, Miss Brande, you
will be on board by eleven to-morrow—
and Marmaduke, too?   Good-night.'

'What!' cried the General next morning, 'not engaged, Cecil, after last night?'
'Certainly not.   It was a pure accident.'
'Now, don't you be a fool.   Don't show
the white feather.   Ask her again.   Bless
my soul! what is a woman's "no"?   They
never like to surrender at the first sum-
mons.   'Tis a point of honour to hold out.
She let poor Dick see clearly enough, what
we all see, that you cut him out.   Besides,
she's bound to give in now, you see.   Last
night's business was compromising.   And
you are bound to bring it to the point at
once.   Confound you, Cecil! a young
fellow didn't want backing up in my time.
There were no laggards in love or war in
my days.   'Twas the curb we wanted, not
the spur, by George!   And such a girl!
Beauty, wit and gold, as the old song says.
Heaven knows when you'll have a better

opportunity for pressing the siege. I proposed to your dear mother in many a worse place. Once in crossing the Channel; unluckily, she was too ill to think of anything but the stewardess then. Once at the opera. Once between the acts of private theatricals : some scoundrel had the curtain raised at the critical moment— too bad! for she'd have had me then if she hadn't been in such a rage at the titters of the audience. The last time 'twas on the top of Milan Cathedral. She thought the view fine ; so did I, for I was looking straight in her face. By George, sir! you take after your mother to that degree. I believe you want nearly as much asking as she did.'

Cecil replied that there never would be any question of marriage between them, since neither of them wished it.

'Your mother and I know better,' his father returned.

'Well, sir,' said Cecil, with sudden recklessness, in view of the inevitable plunge, 'suppose that I can't ? Suppose that I am married already ?'

'Suppose the devil is sky-blue !' retorted the General, marching off to his earthworks in the kitchen garden.

A week later Cecil received a letter enclosing his last to Renée from the head of his wife's school near Orleans, a place he had selected as quieter than Paris and for the purity of its French accent, and whither she had just returned to school for her last *semestre*, taking the child with her. The fine French handwriting, though so familiar to him, was difficult to read, or was it that his eyes were dim ? He had that very day chosen a suitable and pretty home for his wife. He was slowly awakening to the obligations he had taken on himself, not only towards her, but also towards that unwelcome helpless third, the torch of whose frail life had been kindled at his own, and who had hopes and rights for which he was responsible. His face changed as he read on with horror and incredulity ; he grew dizzy ; there was a film over his eyes. He read it a second time ; there was no mistake. But to make quite sure he read it aloud in a strained, unusual voice, like the choked voice of one in a nightmare.

Then he took up an evening paper and read a few columns without knowing what he read. His ears were full of a humming sound, something like the distant roar of leagues of surf. He was thinking of some arrangements contemplated for his wife's comfort in the home destined for her, when on a sudden he fell with a crash to the ground.

His wife and child had been in the burning church ; their charred remains had already been committed to the common grave made necessary by circumstances.

END OF VOL. I.

BILLING AND SONS, PRINTERS, GUILDFORD.